BEYOND THE WALL

BY

BOB COLLIER

PREFACE

Eric Middleton, a seventeen year old youth
from a village in Derbyshire, by some freak of
nature has the ability to travel back in time with
the artefacts he has uncovered with his metal
detector. Experiencing lives of people through
the centuries, and adopting himself into their
ways of life. Finding himself in dangerous
situations, including the Peninsular War against
the French, the battle of Bosworth, and many
more skirmishes, Eric finally settles down in the
twelfth century.

CHAPTER ONE

Eric Middleton was on his knees, not in church praying, but in the middle of a field. It was the latter part of October, clear skies. The sun shone but there was a nip in the air. His fingers were cold from rubbing soil off the coin he had uncovered with his metal detector.

So intense was his passion for detecting, he would close his eyes whilst rubbing, and imagine the bearer of the lost coin, their dress, habitat and so forth, as clear as if he were actually there.

Eric was seventeen years old; he lived with his parents in a modest house in a small village in Derbyshire. The area had been prosperous at one time. The potteries and coal mines were all gone now, and very little trace was left to say they had been there at all.

Unemployed, the future looked bleak for him. The ever-present threat of a nuclear war was the daily topic on everyone's lips. 2020 was not a good time for Eric. The newspapers were full of countries boasting their power; all were at loggerheads as to total disarmament. It didn't seem to matter to Eric, if it came it came, at least he wouldn't have to stand in the queue alongside other hopefuls, seeking a job – any job – that would give him some sort of independence and pride in his life.

He put the old penny coin in his finds pouch, the only artefact he had found all day. Deciding to call it a day, he began walking back to his car, which was parked in the farmyard adjacent to the field. It was agreed by Bill Williams and himself, that anything of value found on his land, would be divided. "However" finds classed as treasure, had to be recorded and logged with The Local Finds Liaison Officer of the area.

Sometimes, better finds were detected on that last walk of the day when you head back home, swinging from left to right, hoping to find that one pot of gold that would set you up for life. Dreaming as he slowly walked away, he listened for that strong defining signal.

As he came to the edge of the field, he picked up a signal; it became stronger in deep undergrowth entwined with brambles. Setting aside his machine and haversack, he began to clear the area with his spade. After what seemed like ages, Eric began pulling out pieces of what looked like railway lines, coke, and chunks of coal; finally a large hole appeared. Even with the farmer's permission, Eric still looked nervously from side to side, to see if anyone was watching him.

Without a torch or some kind of light, Eric could not begin to explore further. He decided to investigate some other time. Concealing the hole as best he could, out of his bag he withdrew a wooden peg, used for marking the area he was detecting on, and pushed it into the ground. Satisfied at his efforts at concealment, he picked up his spade, machine and his bag, and made his way out of the field.

"Had a good day love?" his mother said as he entered the kitchen.

"Not really, just one old penny," he replied.

Later that evening alone with his thoughts, Eric set about planning the next day's event.

His first port of call that morning would be the Local District Council offices, to see if he could study a local Ordinance Survey map of the area, and secondly to the Library to find what past activity, if any, was recorded in that field and its surroundings.

The results of both visits fuelled Eric's imagination even more. A coal mine used to operate close to the field some fifty years ago, and more interesting for Eric, being a detector buff, a Roman road once ran parallel to the field; now all that was left was a ditch. The said field saw plenty of past activity, it was rumoured that there could well have been a Deserted Medieval Village close by.

Eric's mind raced with all this newly acquired information and he could not wait to explore that field again, particularly that intriguing hole. There was no time left today – he had spent most of it in town.

Rarely an early riser, Eric made an exception the next morning, catching his father before he set off for work. He asked his dad if he could borrow his inspection lamp.

"What do you want with that?" his dad asked.

"Just to look for something in the attic," Eric replied.

His dad gave a nod of approval, and Eric went to get the lamp from the garage. It needed new batteries; he had plenty of spare ones he used for his metal detector. The lamp was ideal, more like a mini hand-held searchlight.

After breakfast, he made up a flask of coffee, took a few biscuits and stuffed them in his bag. This time he informed his mum that he was going detecting in the same field he had been for the past few days. His mum knew the field he was talking about.

"What time will you be home?" she asked.

"Just before tea," Eric replied.

He arrived at the farm around 9 a.m., parked his car, and began to trudge across the field towards the wooden marker. The weather was dry, a clear sky, Eric's heart beat faster, a mixture of excitement and apprehension; the nearer he got to the wooden marker. He began to uncover the hole, pushing his items in first before crawling in on hands and knees. Slowly, he entered the dark interior. Just enough light filtered through the opening for him to see, and he found he could stand up if he took a few steps in.

Taking the lamp out of his bag, he switched it on. After letting his eyes adjust to the light, Eric was amazed at what confronted him: a tunnel that declined gradually away, with a high roof supported by intermittent steel rings. The roadway was roughly eight yards wide. Wooden boards shored up the sides. Eric knew he was inside a coal mine drift. Used by miners to haul coal up to the surface by means of a steel rope, or pony. He looked more closely at the floor beneath his feet and found evidence of small railway lines.

Directing the beam of light down the drift, Eric wondered just how far down it actually went. There was only one way to find out. Slowly, he began making his way down. The beam danced from wall to wall, ceiling to floor, following each step. It was a little spooky, Eric thought. The silence was deafening.

What would happen if I had an accident right now? He wondered. The thought was frightening; a cold shiver went through him.

He reached the end some ten minutes later, meeting a wall of stone. He felt he was breathing more rapidly and surmised that the only air here was coming from the small hole he had uncovered. It was colder down here, too, a deep, timeless cold that seeped into his bones.

Satisfying himself he had seen all there was to be seen, he made his way back up the tunnel, feeling a little disappointed.

Puffing and panting, he made it to his equipment; he sat with his back to the wall, and poured himself a coffee from the flask in his bag. He marvelled at the miners who had laboured and sweated to dig this coal out of the ground.

Composed with the hot coffee inside him, he closed his eyes and started day-dreaming again. Eric's personal theory on the passage of time was that they were layered like seams of coal – much like the seams of coal those old miners had followed underground. The evidence came to the surface in the form of the artefacts he detected. To Eric, the past was still underground, and could be mined just like coal.

He shone the lamp on his watch: '11 a.m.' it read.

Five more minutes here, and I guess I'll do a spot of detecting up top, Eric mused to himself. Eyes closed and unaware of the ancient coin in his hand, he stood up against the wall. A peculiar feeling swept over Eric, it seemed as if something was pulling him back, drawing him through the wall. The force was overwhelming. It was like nothing he had ever experienced before.

Terrified as he was, Eric opened his eyes and the effect stopped. Sweating and shaking, he adjusted to the familiar surroundings of the drift.

There had to be a simple explanation as to what just happened, Eric thought, but what?

It had been like a giant magnet pulling his body and soul through the wall. What would have happened if he had let it continue? Just kept his eyes shut and let the force take him?

Totally bewildered and scared, Eric quickly grabbed his bag, detector and spade, and pushed himself out of the hole. Fresh air eased his panic, and dazed, he began to close off the entrance.

What if the experience was real? He thought. *Or was it just my imagination? If it was real, could I make it happen again?*

All ifs. They rattled around his head.

Eric was faced with an uncertainty that filled him with both excitement and fear.

Do I have the nerve and determination to try? Eric asked himself.

Sleep that night eluded him and by morning he had made up his mind to go back to the drift. What puzzled Eric most as he picked at his breakfast was the discrepancy he had noticed on his watch the day before. It had said '11 a.m.' before it happened, but had read midday when he had climbed back out.

Somewhere, he had lost an hour.

Putting the penny in his pocket, Eric informed his mum that he was going to the Job Centre to see if there were any jobs on offer.

Arriving at the entrance to the hole around 9 a.m., trembling with fear and apprehension, he crawled through. He had no lamp today, but enough daylight came through to enable Eric to find the exact place in which to position himself – the same spot he had been the day before.

Standing with his back to the wall he took the coin out of his pocket with trembling fingers. He hesitated, wondering whether he was dealing with some kind of evil. Deciding that there was only one way to find out, he closed his eyes and began to rub the coin.

The same pulling force began behind his navel. Keeping his eyes tightly shut, he felt a queer sensation, as if he was doing cartwheels backwards. Then, as quickly as it had started, it stopped. Eric sensed he was now lying down, his eyes still closed, the penny clutched in his sweating hand. Had he fainted, he wondered? He seemed to be lying down, yet he felt no pain... Was he still in the drift?

Brilliance pierced his eyelids. Slowly he opened his eyes. Blinking in amazement, he realised he was looking up at the sun.

Shielding his eyes, sat up and looked around. He was sitting in the same field, he observed, yet it appeared different. Half of it was ploughed, and at the far end he saw two Shire horses attached to a plough. Behind them, a man was holding long reigns. The farm looked the same but smaller. He also picked out the steeple of the village church in the distance. Instinctively he pinched himself, surely he was dreaming! No, he felt the pinch. On his right hand side should have been the hole, but there was none.

Frantically, he tore away the undergrowth, but found nothing; how was he going to get back?

If I can get back, that is.

Making a mental note of where he was lying, Eric stood up. Putting the penny back in his pocket, found he was wearing old fashioned trousers, leather boots, and an old, smelly shirt. Eric's mind raced: he had somehow slipped into a different period of time, and it had also changed his appearance.

The man and the plough were getting nearer. He waved to Eric.

At least I am not invisible, he thought to himself, and waved back. I need to sort out this phenomenon or whatever it is that has happened to me, and quick.

Eric started walking towards the man, keeping to the edge of the field. The plough was being turned around to begin a fresh furrow when he approached.

"Do you work for Bill Williams?" Eric said, pointing to the farm.

"Aye, I do," he replied, in a strong Derbyshire accent, "but its Sid not Bill, don't know any Bill."

He looked Eric up and down. "Are you from this neck o' the woods?"

"Yes, not far from here," Eric replied.

"Why haven't you been called up?" the ploughman asked.

"Called up for what?" Eric responded.

"This bloody war, what else?" said the man. "You're only exempt if you work in yonder pit, or you're a farmer, which one is it lad?"

Not giving it much thought, Eric blurted out that he was seventeen, and was at the pit, and his day off. The man gave him a strange look, as if he didn't believe him.

"There are rumours of opening up a drift hereabouts, but I reckon it's just talk," he said. "Although, the life of yonder pit has not many more years in it, so they tell me."

With that, he clicked his tongue and the plough began moving forward. Eric was now even more confused what war? He pulled out his penny to see the date, '1939'.

I reckon it's the Second World War, he thought, *but what year am I in?*

Putting the coin back in his pocket, Eric began walking towards the farm, head down and deep in thought. He needed more evidence, he decided. The farm looked a bit smaller than he remembered on nearing the yard, but he'd never actually seen the farm. The only time he'd visited it was to ask permission from Bill Williams to detect on his land.

Leaving the farm, Eric headed towards the village of Skelton. Normally, it would only take him a few minutes by car from home to farm, passing known landmarks, but now he had a job finding his way home. He recognised two old thatched cottages as he came to the end of this particular stretch of road, and near them a shop of some sort.

A newspaper bulletin board was outside: 'Careless talk costs lives', was the headline. The year, when he took a closer look, was 1940.

I have travelled back in time eighty years.

Eric could not believe it. He felt numb and ridiculous, as if this would all turn out to be a joke, but the first piece of evidence was here. He felt as if by some freak of nature, he shouldn't be here. He had no local money apart from the penny in his pocket, and that would not buy him a drink. Eric was suddenly thirsty, either from shock or the hot sunny day.

Realizing that his house would not have been built yet, he decided it would be a waste of time looking for the road, if the road even existed in 1940. Eric looked in the shop window: there were items on display whose names he had never heard of, soap powders, cocoa, liquid coffee in a bottle, tea, and bundles of firewood. Out of curiosity he entered the shop. It was packed with all sorts of oddments for such a small shop. He ducked out of the way of a hanging coil of sticky gummed fly paper, buckets, mops, and an assortment of brushes.

Some of the items he recognised from visiting a local museum somewhere in the larger town. His thoughts were interrupted by an old lady wearing a white apron.

"Can I get you something, me duck?" she said.

"No thanks, just looking," replied Eric.

"We don't have much in the way of food stuff, due to this awful war," she remarked, looking tired and sad at the same time "When will it ever end?

Eric new the answer, of course, but couldn't tell her. Spending a further few minutes looking around, he left the shop. Head bent, fascinated by what he had just seen, he walked back the way he had come. Standing outside of the farm house looking at the front door, he was tempted to knock on the farmer's door, who he now knew was Sid, and say "You will have a son and you will name him Bill." He would most probably suspect Eric was after a few coppers by telling fortunes. He quickly dismissed the thought, and moved on.

Avoiding the ploughman, Eric made his way back to the spot he hoped would take him home.
Please God, let it happen, or I'll die here before I am born, he thought, a shiver going through him.

Lying down, he retrieved the penny and held it firmly in his hand. Eyes closed, he began to rub the coin with his fingers. Blackness encased him, the same tumbling experience made his head swim, and then stillness. Praying like he had never prayed before, Eric opened his eyes. He was back. Strange as it seemed, the drift felt like home.

He groped his way out of the hole, and stood up, it was pitch black, night time. Looking at his luminous digital watch, he saw that it read 11.30 p.m.

Blinking heck, he thought. *I have almost lost a day, never mind an hour!*

Making his way back to his car, he felt elated and glad to be alive, and back in 2020.

Arriving home, Eric let himself in, trying to be as quiet as he could. He went straight to the kitchen. Hungry and very thirsty, began to make himself a sandwich and a well-earned mug of tea.

"Is that you Eric?" his mum bellowed from the top of the stairs. "Where the hell have you been?"

He apologised for being late and waking her up. His excuse was simple: he'd met some mates, took in a film at the cinema, and had a few cans. He could have said, "I was in a local shop that doesn't exist, and in the middle of the Second World War," but she never would have believed him.

CHAPTER TWO

Bewildered and excited, Eric began piecing together the events of his trip back in time.

I could be the only one in the whole world that this has happened to, he thought.

He'd read about people 'seeing the light', or having a near death experience, and of course the stories in fiction books, but to actually have it happen to him was an awesome feeling. He so much wanted to tell the world, his mum, and his mates, but they wouldn't believe him, unless they went to see for themselves on his next trip.

No, Eric said to himself, this is my secret and mine alone.

It occurred to him that he hadn't thought of going back again until then, but knowing he could do it was like that magnet feeling he had experienced in the drift, drawing him in. He pondered why his clothes had changed, and how he'd had the ability to communicate easily in the dialect of the period. Derbyshire slang was easy, but would it change in other time periods.

If he had known in advance, he would have taken more of his old pennies for a drink. He considered the ifs and buts of returning. If he went back he had to be better prepared. What if the ploughman had noticed his modern watch, 'which hadn't vanished? And made a comment, how would he have explained it? He couldn't take anything through that was not of the period.

Which raised the question of how far back could he go? The penny had put him in 1940, a fairly safe period, but what if he was in the middle of a war zone?

Eric began looking through his biscuit tin. It contained all his found objects. Sifting through, came across a lead musket ball. Now that could have been lost in any of two to three different centuries. The ball, unlike others he had found, had tooth marks embedded in it. His books on this subject had explained the meaning of the marks, narrowing down the range. The musketeer placed the ball in his mouth while the musket was being primed with powder, and then spat it down the barrel.

Tossing it from hand to hand, Eric deliberated the chance of going back again.

I have nothing to keep me hear, except my mum and dad, who I may never see again, and they would be worried sick on my absence he thought.

However, the chance of ending up in a conflict was much greater than before. If he was careful, though, he could come back home from God knows where. Explaining his absence to his parents was not going to be easy, particularly knowing that the longer he was spirited away, the greater period of time lapse occurred.

Eric conjured up a story that he was going camping with his mates, and would be away for a few days, but if the weather took a turn for the worse he could be back earlier. Likewise, he told his mates that he was visiting relatives with his parents.

Checking and re-checking, he made sure that the only item on his person was the musket ball. No watch, nothing that would cause an embarrassing situation. He said his goodbyes to his mam and dad, and, clutching his bag of camping kit, left the house.

Will this be the last time I see them? He thought? Feeling a little upset and scared.

With one last look at his home, he began to walk the distance to the farm. Leaving the car parked up at home seemed the right thing to do. Bill Williams might get suspicious seeing it parked in the yard for days, so lumbered with the unnecessary burden of his camping kit, Eric stealthily made his way to the hole.

Dumping the kit on the floor, he stood against the now familiar wall, the musket ball clenched in his hand. Eric decided, as his body reacted to the process, was the bit he didn't like very much. It was a bit like going under general Anaesthetic and counting backwards. Opening his eyes, he sat up quickly, taking in the surroundings.

"Well, no farm this time," he said aloud.

There was just a homestead of sorts. The spire of the church was still visible, but it would be as it had been there since the twelfth century. The field he was standing in was now pasture, not ploughed.

Eric stood up, eager to see what transformation had occurred to his state of dress, hoping to get some inkling as to what period he was in, started at his feet, and worked up. Old black boots again, no laces. Grey breeches half way up his legs, which were torn and grubby. An off-white large shirt with sleeves so wide you could fit five arms in them at once. Braces that were holding up the breeches by only three buttons, and a leather belt around his middle.

Eric thought that he looked like something out of Oliver Twist, late seventeenth or early eighteenth century, maybe. His thoughts were interrupted by a volley of bangs some distance away, which instinctively made him crouch down. Gun shots.

"Christ," Eric blurted out, "I hope they weren't aimed at me!"

After some minutes, Eric stood up. He could see white puffs of smoke dispersing into the blue cloudless sky some four fields away. Making sure he had no holes in the one pocket of his breeches he put the ball safe inside, then without hesitation began to run towards the direction of the village.

More shots were fired. The sounds were fainter now, but Eric kept running, badly out of breath. He paused for a second, only to get his breath back; he was outside the thatched cottages.

They looked newer now than last time he had been here. The road wasn't as wide, just packed hard earth, and full of pot holes, and horse manure in abundance. The houses on either side of the road seemed to be squashed together, if you could call them houses. They were more like 'hovels'. The shop as he remembered it was now an 'ale-house', as the crudely written sign said above the door.

Feeling a little safer now amongst people who looked as if they had come out of a Charles Dickens story, Eric wondered what period he was in. He peered into the public house: so dense was the smoke from tobacco that he could hardly see inside. Men were shouting in a strong Derbyshire accent puffing away on white clay pipes, drinking from pewter and pot mugs. He was considering entering, when he was pushed aside roughly by a tall man. "Gerroutertheer gutter snipe!" he growled, indicating Eric, with a pointing finger. He was dressed differently to those inside, more refined.

"What yo gorpin' at?" the man demanded.

Eric, who was taken by surprise by the sudden outburst, sidestepped to let him pass. In doing so, he stepped into a gutter – one of two that ran either side of the road – filled with foul smelling water, horse manure and what looked like human sewage. The stench of the place was overwhelming.

He was aware of the smell of sewage on his trousers; he didn't think the people would respond to him any differently? As he neared the centre of the village, he noticed a large green with a water pump and trough in the middle. Horses and carts were tethered everywhere. Eric guessed it could be market day; stalls were laid out in a straight line at the edge of the green. Flies were buzzing over a meat stall, next to that, fruit and veg' were on display. The fruit looked only fitting for pigs. There was even a leather stall. All the vendors were shouting at the same time. One in particular, made Eric stop and linger. The woman behind the meat pie stall, gave Eric the once over.

"Ey-up-me-duck," she called. "Little uns ha-penny, big uns a penny!"

Why was it that this time travelling lark gave you a thirst as well as hunger pains? he mused.

"I wouldna if I wos yo mate,"a voice whispered in his ear. "Yo will have yor shoulder felt." Eric was looking at a lad about the same age as himself, more shabbily dressed, black as a chimney sweep from head to toe, and he smelled like the gutters.

"Nabbed by law yo bin," he continued, prodding and winking at Eric. "I can get us one o' them pies fer nowt. Just yo keeps old Pie face talking, and I'll meet thee at end o stalls." Pointing a dirty finger, quick as a flash, he vanished.

Looking at the woman sheepishly, Eric spoke for the first time.

"Can you make them cheaper?"

The woman leaned forward.

"If I wer t- make um cheaper, I'll be gee in um away. Aneroid, I reckons yo ain't got money." Eric plucked up courage to say, "If I asked you to make them cheaper, must mean I have money."

He could feel himself blushing at his own outburst.

27

"Na-then-clever clogs, gerr-outter-theer, else I'll call t-law!" she shouted.

Eric moved away, hoping that that was enough time for the lad to do what he had to do, and sauntered away to the end of the stalls.

True to his word, his new friend was waiting for Eric, two small pies concealed in his dirty hands.

"Towd ya, easy!" he grinned. "Let's eat um at water pump, lest be seen."

Still unsure of making conversation, Eric so much wanted to find out details of this scruffy kind hearted lad. Taking a much needed drink from the pump, they set about devouring the meat pie. Through mouthfuls, Eric asked what his name was, how old he was, and where he was from.

"Me proper name be Tom, but hereabouts they call me 'a thieving dirty bugger'," he told him. "I'm from the city of Derby," he went on. "I reckon I be about seventeen, or thereabouts."

"Why did you leave home?" Eric pushed Tom into replying.

"Too many mouths to feed at Om, so I's left."

Poor sod, Eric thought. And I thought I had it bad on the dole.

Tom didn't like all these questions. It clearly made him uncomfortable and he switched the conversation back to Eric.

"How com yo is clean and that, and good wi' words?"

Eric explained that he washed in the brook, a mile or two back, and made up a story of leaving his home, and was educated by his dad, who was a clergyman. That seemed to satisfy Tom.

"I think it a waste o time washin, yo only gets black agin. Do you have any pennies?" asked Tom.

Eric just shrugged.

"I does odd jobs in't village," he said. "Makes a few coppers, like emptying slop buckets from ouses, yo know. Shit and piss should empty in't dunny out back, but for quickness, ar tosses em inta gutter."

"Do you wash your hands after?" Eric asked, thinking of the pies in his dirty hands.

"I weshes um here at pump," Tom replied simply. Eric spluttered, he had just drunk from the pump.

I hope to God my childhood inoculations are still valid in this period of time, he thought, and shuddered with it.

After resting from their nourishment, Eric looked back to the end of the green, some hundred yards or more away, where people were gathering.

"What do you think's happening over there?" he asked Tom.

"Recruiting fer Army," the lad said. "Com on, let's head on down, and have a shufters," Tom urged Eric.

They could hear a loud voice shouting, over the top of the din of the crowd, which was now accumulating.

"Gerroutterode," Tom said, pushing aside an older man. "Com on mate," he said to Eric, "let's get t-front."

The speaker was sitting on an empty beer barrel, a crude table in front. He seemed to be a big man, even when sitting; he wore a red tunic, white cross belt, and three gold stripes on his sleeve.

"I am Sergeant Hoskins of his Majesty's Infantry, and our King George the third, is willing to pay you a shilling now, to enlist in the Infantry!" he shouted. "Just step forward and make your mark on this here paper!"

That's not be press ganging," replied Tom, in Eric's ear.

Of course, Eric knew the meaning of press ganging, but played dumb.

"Fancy earning a bob, ere? Wots yo name mate," Sergeant Hoskins called.

"Call me Eric."

The queue was getting bigger.

Eric didn't like this one little bit – he hadn't bargained for this.

"What we do is sign the paper, gets the shilling, then bugger off quick-like," Tom whispered.

"Bloody hell," the Sergeant exclaimed, looking at two urchins in front of him, one clean, and the other looking like a chimney sweep.

"Corporal, this un here needs a bass broom," pointing a finger at Tom, "a good scrubbing from head to toe!" The Sergeant bellowed at the man standing next to him, who eyed Tom up in a dubious manner.

"Yo canna do that, thall-catch-me-death-o-cowd," Tom shouted back.

Having a good number of recruits standing before him, the Sergeant dismissed the onlookers, and began his speech to the men and young boys.

"You will be paid sixpence a day in arrears, clothed and fed, trained, drilled, and learn the art of the musket. The reason you are paid in arrears," he explained. "Is, if you're killed in conflict, which some of you will be, then the government pockets your pay, it's as simple as that. What we have here Corporal," he continued, gesturing to the recruits, "is a bunch of riffraff, thieves, vagabonds, and them who is just grateful for a roof over their heads, food in their bellies, and money in their pockets – if they live long enough that is."

"Straighten up, you lot of women," bellowed the sergeant, "and turn to your right, now that you have made your mark on't paper, you're mine! Quick March!"

Eric felt for the ball in his pocket, which now accompanied his shilling, and wondered how in God's name he had got into this mess. They passed the church, then his field of return, or in his case, the field of no return.

Tom, who was behind Eric, constantly complained about how his feet hurt.

"Shut tha gob, and keep up with rest on um," urged the Sergeant.

"Bet tha din't think it wer gonna be that easy did tha, yo theevin bugger?"a man spat at Tom from behind. "Stop yor bloody moanin'!"

They passed several more fields before they turned into one huge one.

"Halt!" the sergeant shouted, and went over to speak to yet another sergeant. They both returned, to face the dusty bedraggled men.

"This 'ere is Sergeant Hollywell, your Instructor, who is your mother, your father and the rest of your bloody family, for the rest of the weeks you are in training."

"Oh-eck," Tom answered to no one in particular, lifting one foot then the other. "Seen him brawling in't village, big bugger ain't he?"

"And' ugly to boot," another replied.

Sergeant Hollywell had a scar running from under his right eye to his chin, catching the corner of his lips.

"I will have to have a few words with the recruiting Sergeant," he spat, "enlisting a pathetic bunch o weasels like you lot. After your training, you will be sent to Portugal – God help us – to fight the French. I got this," he said, pointing to his face, "from a French's sabre, but he died on the end of my bayonet, ripped his belly open like a bag o peas. If any one of you's should be thinking of running away, I will hang you here in this camp, in front of you all, show an example to others."

Each man had to give his name to the Sergeant, as he approached each individual. Looking down at Tom, he sneered, "You must be the dirty smelling bugger, that's in need o' a good scrub."

Lifting Tom off his feet, he dragged him towards a horse trough nearby, and flung him in; two corporals were standing alongside, with hard, coarse brooms. Eric could hear Tom's pleas for mercy as he and others were each given a bedroll, tin mug, a musket, a tinderbox, boots, and pantaloon type trousers, and shown to respective tents.

"Poor old Tom," Eric smiled; he sure as hell, will scarper now that he's clean.

Sitting around a camp fire drinking weak tepid tea, Eric took stock of his surroundings: there were horses tethered to a long, taught rope at the far end of the field, presumably for those who chose the cavalry, row upon row of tents, a large kitchen marquee, and a picket guard at every corner of the field. Eric began to piece together the period he thought he was in: somewhere between 1805 and 1810, Trafalgar he knew was 1805, and what he'd gained at school about the British army in the Peninsula, commanded by 'Lord Wellington' put him, as near as damn it, in 1810.

Tom joined them, grumbling and cursing, mug in hand. Although Eric had only known him for a short time, had grown fond of him.

"I'm gonna git outta this dump," he hissed, voice lowered just for Eric, "easy as slipin' a lock."

"If they catch you," Eric acknowledged, "they will hang you."

"Better to die here than on the end of a French's bayonet in a foreign land," Tom replied, spitting out a mouthful of tea. "Tastes like piss."

Eric urged him to sleep on it.

Eric's second day in transitory began at 05.30, all awoken by a bugle being blasted across the camp. He was pleased to see Tom, lying near him on the floor, snoring his head off. "Tom – Tom! Come on, move your arse!" He shook him violently. "The sergeant's outside, shouting to assemble, on the double!"

Dressing hastily in the given clothes, Eric transferred the musket ball from his trouser pocket to his new white trousers; both made a quick exit from the tent.

"Right you ugly buggers! Get your mugs, and make your way over to the kitchen for breakfast – and I expect to see you here in fifteen minutes to begin musket drill!" yelled the big man.

Eric, Tom and the others lined up. The cook poured stewed tea in the mugs, and ladled a dollop of what looked like porridge onto their plates.

"That will stick to your ribs," the cook chuckled, "and keep the tin plate; it's yours for the duration."

Finding a place to squat around one of many camp fires that were attended day and night, they began to eat their breakfast.

"How can a bloke fight on this shit?" Tom asked, lifting his voice for all to hear. Eric could sense that Tom's sudden outbursts would only bring more hardship to the lad, but said nothing.

They were each given a square back pack, held in place by two white cross belts. House bricks were placed inside; these were to compensate for the many items one had to carry when in conflict. Drill, drill and more drill. They must have passed each corner of the field about twenty times, at a fast running pace. At last, the sergeant was satisfied that they now marched as one troop, in an orderly fashion. After a short rest, it was musket training. Standing out front,

Sergeant Hollywell brandished a musket in his huge hands.

"Listen, and listen well. This here weapon will save your life in a skirmish, if handled correctly."

Eric wanted to blurt out that a modern assault rifle would be better, but he kept his mouth shut.

"The ram rod is here," he indicated the underside of the musket. "That rams everything home."

At his feet was a box of lead musket balls, strips of wadding, powder cartridges, and a horn of black powder – and most important of all, a tinder box.

"This is a flintlock, name of 'Brown Bess', long barrel short stock." He went on to point out the firing mechanism, hammer, with its half cock, and full cock, pan, and frizzen. "Firstly, make sure you have a piece of flint screwed into the hammer. Second, insert a powder cartridge down the barrel, followed by a ball in wadding, then ram 'um down with the ramrod, thus. Lastly, pour a little black powder into the pan, and gentlemen, you have a killing machine.

Kicks like a mule and blackens your face to boot. Your tinder box contains extra flints, wadding, and a small piece of metal. Later, you will be given a leather pouch in which to carry your lead balls, in the meantime, put a handful in your pocket, next to your own balls, keep 'um company, so to speak."

Tom's face showed a picture of delight, when given his musket, powder and balls.

"Could do a lot o damage wi' this!"

"As long as it's at the enemy," replied the sergeant icily.

The targets were straw images, roughly fifty yards away. Tom was the first person ready to fire. Hammer pulled back, awaiting the order of the sergeant to aim and fire.

"Fire!"

The line was just a mist of white smoke, men were flung everywhere from the recoil, only Tom stood firm, grinning. A corporal, who was attending the shoot, could not believe what he saw: only Tom hit the target. After several more attempts, the result was the same. Seeing a potential marksman amongst us, the sergeant took Tom to one side. You look like a candidate for a sniper's role within the Infantry.

"What that be then?" Tom looking sheepishly up at him.

"You work independently of the troop, does the job, then gets out undercover."

"Yo mean I does me job killin', and am me own boss?"

"Yes, something like that," smirked the sergeant.

Moving the straw target further away, roughly eighty yards, Tom was handed a different musket, the barrel being riffled, so the sergeant informed him, and stuck a thin metal rod in the ground, the musket nestling in the 'v' at the top. The sights of this musket could be altered, depending on the distance.

"Right now shoot that Frenchmen lad, when you are ready."

Everyone was talking and taking bets, the whole situation was so tense – and then, *bang* – the musket exploded with a puff of smoke, the French straw head was severed from its body.

At the end of a tiring day, we handed over our muskets to Sergeant Hollywell.

"Let's be having your unused balls as well, he barked, carrying a box."

Each man in turn, dug deep and threw them in the box. Eric's turn arrived, to discard his balls.

"Bloody Hell!" he swallowed hard against the tightness suddenly banded about his throat. "I've mixed my lead ball with the issued ones!"

"Come on lad, haven't got all day," the irritable big man yelled.

He had little choice, but to place them in the box, and watched pitifully as the rest of the men did the same.

How am I going to get home now? Eric thought.

After evening meal, sitting alone with Tom, he explained as much as he dared, referring to the musket ball as a lucky charm, at having the teeth marks and all that.

"I have to find it Tom," he said, anxiety building up in the tone of his voice.

"They be hundreds o' them little buggers int' box'," Tom said, giving little encouragement.

"I have to sort through them, right now."

Crawling out of the tent, he walked over to the box – gratefully left on the firing line – and began to empty the shot in a heap on the ground. One by one, he carefully examined each ball before placing them back into the box.

This is going to take forever, he thought.

"What do you think yo be doing?" asked a piquet guard standing over Eric.

"I was ordered to make sure each man had enough balls for practice tomorrow," Eric stammered, "and I forgot to do it earlier."

Satisfied with his remark, the guard walked away, leaving Eric to continue his search. What seemed like hours later, knees hurting from kneeling so long, Eric found the ball. Well, he hoped to God it was the one. Returning to his tent, he made up his mind to leave this very night. He would miss the banter and company of the recruits, but he could not stay to be drafted. The thought of never getting back from Portugal made him sweat with fear.

Tom, however, seemed to have found his purpose in life as a sniper, and spoke of nothing else, eager to be useful, and proud to have been picked.

Leaving in just the clothes he arrived in, Eric made his way stealthily to the spot where the drift mine would be dug in a few centuries time, a few fields away. Looking back for the last time, seeing the glow from the night fires and thinking of Tom and the others sleeping, he lay down, ball in his hand. He closed his eyes, rubbed the musket ball and prayed.

Dumping his camping kit in the hallway, Eric made for the kitchen.

"I'm starving!" he said to his mother, after saying hello.

"Was the weather that good then?" she said, whilst preparing dinner. "You've been gone weeks." We were thinking of going to the police and record you missing; both me and your dad were frantic with worry.

"What's for dinner? He asked.

"Your favourite, steak and kidney pie," she replied.

Eric smiled, thinking of Tom, and those meat pies in his black hands.

CHAPTER THREE

Eric decided to give travelling a miss for a while, and spend more time with his parents, which was easy, considering he had no job. His dad was constantly urging him to get out and look for work, knowing full well how the situation was. His mother on the other hand, liked having Eric at home.

"He keeps me company," she would say. She was a bit soft-hearted, and not really understanding the frustration he was going through. It wasn't long before boredom set in again for Eric.

Spending weeks in his bedroom, reading, and contemplating his past adventures, the latter giving him a tingle of self-satisfaction. To merely rub his fingers and be bodily transported into another dimension, now that was something. Reading a good book gave you the opportunity to be in the story, but only in mind – but to be actually there and involved, to Eric, it was mind boggling.

Actually Eric could keep going back until he died, in this decade, or even earlier. What he regretted the most, was the ageing process of his parents, his time spent away, leaving him just a little older on his return home.

The answer, Eric thought, *is to leave home permanently, and correspond by a telephone call when I get back from my travels.*

He told his mum and dad that he had got a job in Germany, labouring on a building site. His mam was distraught, but was consoled by his dad saying, "At least he has a job."

Informing the DWPS that he had obtained the job on line, was straight-forward. Getting rid of his car was no problem. He put the money he got from the car, plus money he had saved whilst on the dole, into the inside of a book, ironically named 'Gulliver's Travels'.

'Where, and when?' That was the question on Eric's mind.

Tipping out all his odds and sods from his biscuit tin onto the bed, he smiled at the musket ball.

I wonder if Tom died here in Skelton, or on the battle field in Portugal, Eric thought. *He never did give his surname, otherwise I could look him up in the local graveyard.*

Brushing the thought aside, Eric picked up a piece of a tamper (used for bedding down tobacco in a pipe). Intact, it would have a flat image of King Charles I or second. His reference books dated it to around 1625 but he only had the metal stem of the tamper.

I wonder, Eric thought. *Would this take me through?*

After his last travels, Eric came to the conclusion that he hadn't study the period well enough, so, with his laptop, he began in earnest to gather as much information on the sixteenth century as possible. He discovered that he could go into the English Civil War, toward the end of the reign of King Charles the first, or the Restoration of his son, Charles the second. The first being hounded by the Parliamentarians, under Oliver Cromwell, the second, part of the turmoil of England recognising Charles the second.

Surely, a little village like Skelton wouldn't witness much of those activities, Eric thought. *Cities, yes...*

To Eric, both periods sounded exciting, his fate was in the tamper.

Catching a taxi from home, he told his parents that he was going to the airport, and that he would see them in a few months time. The driver dropped Eric off at the bottom of the lane leading to the farm; it was evening, so he hoped he wouldn't be seen by anyone. Arriving at the drift, Eric checked his holdall: money, laptop, and a good supply of clothes, the latter needed when he returned, and had to find lodgings in Derby. He had purposely grown his hair longer than normal, along with a few days growth of beard, thinking he would blend in better in the period.

Would this piece of tamper be enough to take him through?

"Oh well, no turning back now," he said, aloud.

He knew it had worked, finding himself, a few minutes later, lying down in a wet pasture, eyes still closed, aware of hot smelling breath on his face.

"Christ," he blasphemed to himself, "Looks like I'm going to have a sword through my ribs before I've bloody well started."

After a second, the hot breath moved from his face He dared to open his eyes to greet the executioner, squinting through one eye, made out a black shiny nose. Eyes now fully open, he realized a sheep was standing over him. Sitting up, the sheep suddenly bolted with Eric's movement.

Heart rate slowing down, he stood up and looked around at his surroundings. The hedgerows were replaced by dry stone walling, some four feet high, looking towards the church. He noted that the farm was no longer there.

Would the village be gone as well? Eric thought.

He was just about to walk over to the church when the ground beneath his feet shuddered, the sound of galloping horses were getting nearer to where he stood. He concealed himself by sitting with his back to the wall – they were getting closer, a few minutes and they would be upon him. One, two, three horsemen, one after another, jumped over the wall, showering Eric with mud and uprooted grass tufts. They galloped towards the church. . Eric stood and peered over the wall, no more horsemen followed, thank God.

After this scary encounter, he took in his appearance.

"Not again," Eric said to himself. "Why does it put me in a lower class of dress? Just for once, I would like to be attired in the clothes of the nobility clothes. Is it because I am out of work, a 'nobody' in my normal life, or does time think I stand a better chance of survival in these clothes?"

His feet were covered in soft, felt type slippers. He had on brown woollen hose, a brown leather jacket, and high collard white shirt. Making the tamper safe in his jacket pocket, Eric started to walk towards the church, looking over his shoulder at intervals in case there were other riders following.

By the time he reached the church, his feet were soaking wet.

"Stupid bloody shoes," Eric grumbled to himself.

Trudging along the village road, which had altered very little (though there were more pot holes and it was narrower), in the distance he could make out the green, the odd houses scattered here and there – presumably farm

49

workers dwellings – and the village tavern, which now had three horses tethered outside. The two thatched cottages were gone, replaced by a blacksmith's forge.

The forge was open fronted; Eric noticed the smithy banging and hammering inside, a stable yard was to the side. The man looked a typical blacksmith: huge arms, moustached, his black hair tied back by a ribbon of sorts. Conscious of his stupid appearance, made worse by being splattered with mud, Eric chanced a meeting with this man. Crossing the rutted dirt track of a road, Eric was quickly rehearsing a story in his mind. The man looked up, pausing in his work.

"You will have to wait a while, afore I get around to shoeing your horse," the big man said. Eric found the dialect difficult to understand at first, not like the Derbyshire he was used to.

"My horse threw me a mile back, and bolted," Eric lied convincingly.

The man looked him over.

"You don't seem wealthy enough to have a horse, and to top that, you ain't got no sword, no dagger, nowt to defend thyself, so what's your game?"

"I was a stable boy for a nobleman in Lichfield," Eric lied. "He wasn't a fair man, so I took a horse, and was heading for Derby, hoping to find work."

Eric was pleased with his sudden tale; he was getting quite good at lying.

''They'll hang yer for that," the man said.

"Not if they don't have the evidence – I mean horse," Eric corrected himself, quickly. "Anyway, most likely it's galloped back to that miserable git."

"Well, if you don't want shoeing, a sword, or a pikestaff, I can't offer you owt else – except water in that pail, to wash the mud offer your face."

Taking up the man's offer, Eric began washing off the mud, the water smelled like urine, most probably was.

"What work are you seeking then?" the smith asked, speaking whilst he resumed the task of shaping a shoe.

"Anything' Eric mumbled, wiping his face on a piece of dirty, rough cloth.

"Times are hard nowadays, what with the passin' o' that bloody stupid war, and since the Lord Protector died, folks don't know if they be coming or going. We lives in fear so we do, lives in fear."

Eric studied the man as he was working and talking: he guessed his age to be thirty maybe a little more, young to own a forge, perhaps his parents died in the war. He was tall and heavy set, with bulging biceps. His manner was pleasant. There was something of a twinkle in those blue eyes – underneath that tough exterior, a teddy bear lurked.

"Not much meat on yer." he observed, looking at Eric. "Thin as a lath – reckon a day's hard labour would see yo in't grave. How about you working these bloody bellows for me?" he asked, after a moment. "Yer can have a floor in't attic, and I'll give you grub. No coins, bit scarce at present. What do yer say?"

Eric nodded.

Could be worse, he thought.

Numerous shoes later, eyes red and streaming from the heat and fumes, Eric was totally knackered.

"Have a break lad, water's in't barrel, indicating to the far side of the forge."

Eric had never been more grateful in his whole life, as he was now, just for water.

"While your tekin' a break, nip down t' tavern, and tell Molly her needs to do three dinners," said the blacksmith. "Molly's my daughter, works for that arsehole of a landlord at' tavern."

Glad of being outside, away from that fire, Eric was suddenly struck with the smell of the village. Above him, dark clouds threatened rain. It was dry now, but later the road would be ankle deep in mud, piss, and shit – the brown flow, foul with its corrosive stench. The three horses were still tethered outside. Eric paused before entering, not too sure of himself.

I have to be more assertive, he decided. After all, I am now part of the village. No more lying, for the time being, that is.

So, gathering his composure, Eric went inside. The three soldiers were sitting at a long table, cheese and bread on pewter plates and pewter mugs of ale before them. The din of conversation and merriment stopped suddenly, all eyes were on Eric, and, feeling embarrassed, and blushing from his toes to the top of his head, he noticed the only girl in the room, and made his legs move forward towards her.

"Are you Molly?" he stammered.

"Who be askin'?" this young, beautiful girl said to Eric. "Your dad asked me to tell you that three dinners were to be made today. And it's Eric that's asking."

"Well Eric," she teased, "tell my dad, I'll be home shortly."

Eric retreated slowly away. As he passed by the three men, one spat a nugget of phlegm onto the floor.

Dirty bastard, Eric said to himself.

It began raining as he headed back to the forge and, sure enough, the stench became worse. He was deep in thought, as he tried to side step the filth. In ancient Rome for instance, and in this country, the Romans had great systems of aqueducts, sewers, and plumbing – what went wrong? All it took was water sanitation, now all those years later, here in 1665 it was just a pile of shit, and it would be until the early nineteenth century. Eric smiled to himself, from the beginning of time to the nineteenth century, this planet was covered by a layer of shit. But with it came terrible diseases – the average life span here was thirty, if you didn't die by the bullet or sword, or another weapon, you certainly died of a disease, and were forgotten.

Reaching the forge was happy to dry himself off by the fire.

"Did you see our Molly?" the smithy enquired.

"Yes, no problem," replied Eric, pumping the handle of the bellows. Later in the day, he was shown the room in the attic. There was no furniture, just a wooden make-shift bed that looked on the small side, and a few blankets on top.

Descending the narrow rickety stairs, Eric was puzzled as to where the blacksmith and Molly slept. Molly had arrived, and was in the kitchen, cauldron clattering, knife chopping on wood.

"Sounds like her be back," Molly's dad said. "Good cook our Moll is, when her has owt to put in't pot for a meal'. I'll tidy up in't shop, go see if her needs owt doin' in't kitchen."

Eric obeyed, and went into the back room. The kitchen was sparse of furniture: there was a three seater wooden settle on one wall. In the middle of the flagstone floor was a rough old oak table and four chairs, two pewter candlesticks in the middle. At the far end was a black iron stove, similar to a range; the walls were of white washed brick. Molly looked up, as Eric approached.

"It's about time dad had help in't forge, works too hard he does. So Eric, where you from?" she asked, slicing carrots, potato and turnips, then proceeding to dice fatty mutton. Turning her back on Eric, she placed all of it in a big black pot on the stove. Eric began to tell the same tale he told her dad.

The only girls Eric got involved with were those at the disco in town, or those in the local pub, always with his mates. He felt clumsy and embarrassed, not finding the right words to say to them, frustrated at being a virgin, an oddity given the period he lived in. He noticed Molly's chapped red hands, long eyelashes, blue-green eyes and long brown curls under her white mop cap. He had never been so close like this to a girl, but she seemed different, with a happy-go-lucky attitude. Eric was more relaxed in her presence.

"Do you want any help?" he offered.

"Everything's in hand," she replied.

He excused himself, and left by a side door, which he found himself in the courtyard. Again, the stench overpowered him, mainly coming from the stables and the privy at the rear of the building. Four horses eyed him up, heads emerging over the half stable doors. Eric stroked one's muzzle, and was amazed at how soft it felt. They were big animals, like shire horses, used for farm work and pulling large wooden carts or drays. He made his way to the rear of the yard, chickens clucking around his feet, then it hit him, the urge to vomit overpowered him, the stench was indescribable.

Hand over his mouth, Eric made his way to the privy, stepping over all manner of shit, chicken, dog and human. The privy was a crude small shed, a small diamond shape was cut into the door at the top, gently opening it, he peered in, a frenzy of flies and rats scurried out. A plank with a hole in the centre, over a dug pit in the ground, torn out pages from a book littered the floor, and husks from corn, the shit nearly touched the top of the plank. Eric closed the door quickly, stepped back, and took in the scene of filth. To his left was a huge dung pile, and evidence of where the privy was before, obviously they moved it when it was full. Not fifty yards away was a running stream, common sense will tell you, that the dung heap would seep into the stream, and be carried down to the next village. If this was their only water supply, God help them.

"Oh, for a peg," Eric mused, as he made his way back to the side door. A different smell came from the kitchen; her dad was sitting on the settle smoking a clay pipe.

"Tekin' the air have yer?" he looked at Eric with a sheepish grin.

"Just looking around," Eric answered.

"Our Moll' tells me, your name be Eric. Mine's Samuel, but folks hereabouts call me Sam 'the smith' cause I does most things in't village."

"Grubs up, park yer arses," Molly interrupted her dad, dumping a soot-caked pot on the table.

Sam poured ale from a cask into dented pewter mugs. The smell from the pot was heaven to Eric. As Molly began ladling the contents onto pewter plates, Sam meanwhile, was slicing bread with the same knife he kept on his belt. It was the best meal Eric had eaten in all of his travels, however, as it went down, he was constantly reminded that what went in had to come out, and the need to use the privy later, filled him with dread.

Making conversation, Eric asked Molly where she slept, during a lull at the table.

"Why? Does thy want to take advantage of a poor wench like me, Eric me lad?"

"Not at all!" Eric replied, choking on a piece of mutton.

Sam explained that he slept in the shop next to the furnace, for security purposes – and warm, to boot – and that Molly slept in the stables, mainly for the same purpose. Meal finished, Molly left to work her evening shift at the tavern. Left alone, Sam suggested that Eric go down to the tavern to keep Molly Company, so to speak, and tossed a few coppers onto the table.

"I see you don't carry a knife. Yo have to defend yersen in these 'ere parts," he said, and placed a sheathed knife alongside the money.

Eric thanked him, picked up the knife and pennies, and left the kitchen.

He didn't really want to go, but the thought of Molly being alone with vulgar men filled him with dread. The evening was warm, which made the stench intensify. He managed to glean from Molly both the year and month: September 1665 in the reign of Charles II. He cunningly explained that he had a lapse of memory, due to the fall from his horse.

Molly was pleased to see Eric, as he entered the tavern, and approached Molly who was resting her elbows on the bar counter.

"I ain't exactly rushed off my feet," she said, pointing to the three locals drinking and smoking at a table. "This is Owen, the Landlord, as tight fisted as they come," she said, introducing Eric to a grubby, dishevelled man, standing next to her.

"Yo be grateful I gin yo a job, think yersen lucky yo got a job at all," he grunted. "And I only took yo on 'cause on yer big tits yo half display to customers. Draws 'em in, so to speak."

Molly took his remark with good humour, but Eric wanted to wipe the smirk off his face. Eric had to admit, he liked the look of Molly's huge breasts. Purchasing two tankards of ale, he led Molly to a far corner of the tavern, out of earshot of the three men and Owen. Eric guessed Owen to be about thirty. He was bald, fat, of medium build, with a mouth full of black un-even teeth, bushy sideburns, and a drooping moustache. He took an instant dislike to Owen.

Molly insisted that Eric should talk about himself, which he found difficult, but now had the ability to lie so easily the problem was remembering what he had actually said in previous conversations.

Molly expressed how difficult it was, after her mum died of disease. Being the only child, she had to fill her mother's shoes at a very early age.

"I won't be doing this work for ever," she told him, hitching up her top – which kept sliding down off her bosom every time she gestured with her arms.

"What would you like to do, then?" Eric asked, trying to make Molly do all the talking.

"I would love to work in a big house, as a maid to a noble lady," she grinned. "I'd get to wear nice dresses, and be with a different class, not like the riff-raff in this village. Not including you, Eric luv," she added, giving his hand a squeeze. "You're nothing like this lot around here. You think before you speak, and when it comes out it's nice like."

Without warning, she leaned forward and kissed Eric on the mouth, tantalizing his tongue with hers. Eric was instantly aroused – good job he was sitting down, those stupid tight hose left nothing to the imagination, not like trousers. She smelled of lavender: at this time, most women wore a little cloth bag pinned under the skirt, to hide their odour, filled with smelling herbs, such as lavender, rose petals, rosemary. Eric guessed Molly had one under her skirt.

The three regular drinkers got up, and made to go out, giving Eric the once over as they passed his table, leaving no customers in the tavern.

Molly asked Owen if she could finish early and go home.

"Clear them tables afore yo go then," Owen sneered.

Eric waited for Molly outside, he reckoned it to be about 10 p.m. The stench hit him like a wet flannel, but it was not as pungent as in the day. Molly was outside in a matter of minutes, linking her arm in Eric's. They began walking back to the smithy, side-stepping over all manner of crap on the road.

"You see all this dog shit? Well," Molly exclaimed, "the local tanner pays kids to collect it in a bucket, it softens the leather, so they's tell me."

"Is that so Eric mumbled," touching the leather belt around his waist.

Nearing the Smithy, Molly asked Eric if he would like to visit her boudoir/ stable.

"Sure," he said, thankful for the dark night that hid the colour creeping up his neck. The Smithy was in darkness as they neared; no doubt Sam was tucked up beside the warm forge fire, dreaming of iron. Molly took down an oil lamp from a hook on the wall, lighting the wick with

63

flint in a tinder box, and placing it in a manger. It gave off a warm cosy glow. A large palliasse was placed over clean straw, and Molly began to unlace her bodice. She stepped out of her skirt.

"Come on Eric don't be shy, 'get yer pants off!"

Eric couldn't take his eyes off Molly's breasts, like two melons, nipples sticking out like chapel hat pegs.

"Come on," she said, helping Eric off with his hose. "Do you want me on top, or on me back?"

This was something he had never envisaged so soon in his travels. He made a lunge for Molly's breasts.

"Yo be a tit man then," she grinned, letting Eric fondle and tweak her swollen nipples.

Sensing Eric to be a virgin, Molly lay down and opened her thighs, pulled him gently on top of her, and guided him into the depths of pleasure. Even lying on a palliasse, strands of straw found its way between them, pricking Eric's arse.

A tumble in the hay would have been softer, he thought.

Soon after, Molly was snoring; Eric dressed and made his way out of the stable, gently closing the bottom and top doors, not before covering Molly over with a coarse blanket.

On his bed, alone with his thoughts, Eric was reliving what had just happened. She must have known he was a virgin, with his hesitation and his fumbling, but didn't let on at all; he had had the odd grope and a quick feel with local girls in the pictures, but the pleasure he had found with Molly was awesome.

Eric chuckled to himself, "The first man in 2020 to have shag in the sixteenth century." If he'd told his mates, they would say he'd lost his marbles.

Putting thoughts to one side, tried to get some sleep, but was suddenly conscious of pains and a grumbling in his stomach. After Molly's good dinner and two tankards of ale, the need to have a shit was impending. Fear overtook pains, the thought of finding a candle and tinderbox, and knowing that the privy was full to overflowing, shit curling above the hole in the plank of wood, was too much for Eric. Please let me hold it in until daybreak, closed his eyes and tried to sleep.

He awoke at first light, the cramps still with him. He dressed in the same dirty smelling clothes, descended the old rickety stairs and went out into the courtyard. Outside Molly's stable of passion were piles of small square pieces of hessian, he grabbed a couple. The sun was not up, but the stench from the dung heap and the privy was indescribable. He passed both, holding his breath and pinching his nose, and walked on until he found a decent piece of grass near to the stream. Unbuckling his belt, dropped his hose, and dumped his steaming load. Sighing with relief wiped his arse on the hessian, and covered the mound with stones he gathered beside the flowing stream. Now stripped naked, began washing himself in freezing cold water, he had no option but to put on his clothes whilst being wet. Satisfied with being clean, Eric ambled back to the forge. Nearing the kitchen he smelled food, obviously Molly was cooking breakfast.

"Where as thy bin?" Molly asked, as Eric entered the kitchen.

"Washing myself down by the stream," he replied.

"Sit thysen down, and eat this," she said, thrusting a hot wheat-cake onto his platter. It was a lot like the pancakes his mum made, but thicker. "Yo should use bucket like me and dad uses."

"Well, yes, but it's not the same as having water poured over your body is it?" Eric said, averting his glance away from Molly.

"Wer last night to yer likin' then, Eric me lad?"

Eric just nodded, as Sam entered the kitchen.

"When yo is done eating, get them bellows pumpin, gorra lot on the day," Sam pointed his dagger at Eric, with a piece of wheat cake dangling from the tip.

Eric began day-dreaming as he pumped the bellows.

How can I get Molly to have some sort of shower? He wondered. *I'm sure I could rig something up from all the odds and sods in here, she really hummed last night.In fact, come to think on it, they all pong.*

In the far corner of the shop was a pile of old soldiers' helmets, all dented and misshapen, obviously from the time of the roundheads, here for Sam to melt down. One in particular caught his eye: the wearer must have had a big head since it was the size of a coalscuttle. A shower project was forming in his mind; holes drilled into that helmet would be a good shower head. He remembered reeds growing by the stream, they would make the piping, and all that was needed now was a funnel.

Sam came into the forge some minutes later, and began pushing iron bars into the fire. Having got the fire now white hot, Eric took a breather, taking the time to speak to Sam amid the banging of hammer on iron.

"Could I have one of those helmets that are piled over in the corner?" Eric asked.

"Wot yo want wi' it?" Sam asked, not looking at Eric.

"I have got an idea on how to make a device with running water, so you and Molly can wash under it, a bit like a rain downpour. It will need lots of holes punched into the helmet, and I need a large funnel making." He showed Sam a crude charcoal drawing he had sketched.

With Sam's permission, Eric took a break from the hours of pumping those blessed bellows, and walked down to the stream. He had a quick strip wash, then began to gather different sizes and thickness of reeds. Returning to the yard, he dumped them outside of Molly's stable door, and then headed for the kitchen. On the table he noticed two tankards of frothy ale, presumably Molly had just filled them before going to work. Downing his in one gulp, Eric carried the other through to the forge for Sam.

"Ta, Eric, I needs that," said Sam, gratefully taking the tankard, and – like Eric – downed it in one. "Made that contraption fer ya, and holed thar helmet," Sam proudly said.

"Thanks ever so much Sam," Eric replied, pleased that he had done them so quickly, knowing he had more pressing jobs to do.

Lunch consisted of bread and cheese and of course more ale.

"Slow down, Eric luv, yo will gin yersen pains," Molly stated.

"I need to use my lunchtime to construct the 'contraption'," Eric very nearly said 'shower', but stopped just in time.

Using his knife, Eric began shaving the ends of the reeds, pushing the smaller ones into the bigger, and so on, until he had a sizeable hose.

"What yer mekin', Eric me darlin'?" Molly asked, approaching Eric in the yard.

"You will see soon enough, Molly," Eric said, blushing and beaming all at the same time.

"Bread and cheese is on't table fer yer lunch," she said. "I'm off back to me job, see you at dinner," Molly said, as she sauntered off down the yard.

Eric watched her swinging her hips in a tantalizing way.

"I wonder how she will react when I ask her to take a shower?" he mumbled.

Sam finished work early in the afternoon, which gave Eric the time he needed to set up his shower before Molly returned.

He selected an empty stall next to Molly's, luckily the ground at the back of the stables nearly reached the top of the thatched roof. Dragging the connecting reeds behind him, Eric perched himself on top of the roof, then began to push the hose through the thatch, satisfied on the amount pushed through, made his way down and into the stall.

The hose protruding down was just the right height, and began tying the helmet to the reeds by means of string and the leather chin-strap under the helmet. What he needed now was buckets. He found three shallow wooden ones, they would have to do. Trudging backwards and forwards with water from the stream, Eric placed them close to the hose on the roof. Then he pushed the funnel into the reed, he was ready.

By the time Molly arrived, the water in the buckets would be tepid and not to cold. Sam was first to enter the yard.

"Wot yer stood in't yard fer?"

"Waiting for Molly," replied Eric. "I thought she might like to try my contraption."

Eric took Sam into the empty stall.

"Well," said Eric, pointing to the helmet suspended by the joined reeds.

Sam began to laugh, a chuckle at first, then a raucous belly laugh, Molly appeared in the doorway.

"What's all the fuss about?" she asked, looking at Sam first then to Eric.

"Look yer," Sam pointed to the suspended helmet.

Molly looked up, then fixed her gaze on Eric.

"Explain yersen, Eric me luv."

"Well, this is for you both to have a nice private naked wash," Eric stammered. "Light comes in from the adjoining stalls. Just close the door, stand underneath the helmet, and leave the rest to me. Oh, and you will need, soap, linen-cloths, and a blanket to wrap around whilst you dress. So," he asked them. "Who's first?"

Not to dampen Eric's feelings, Molly agreed to go first. A little later, equipped with the essentials entered the stall, closing the door behind her. Eric raced to the top. In position, he shouted down to Molly, "Are you ready?"

"I am that," came the reply, "and I feel a proper twerp under this helmet."

"Okay, water coming," he called, as he began to pour the first bucket into the funnel.

Amid shrieks of surprise, came pleasurable sounds, mixed with girlish giggles. Nearing the end of his third bucket, Molly shouted that she was finished. Eric and Sam waited for the door to open and out came a clean smelling Molly, her cheeks were rosy, her hair damp.

"Well?" Eric waited with bated breath.

"It wer tingling-refreshing-and luvly – although' it's the first time I have bin pissed on by a Roundhead." She laughed and turned to Sam, "You next!"

The main topic of conversation during dinner was, of course, the shower, one of Sam's remarks was, that it should be open to the village so they could make a few pennies. Eric saw the hard work involved, and quickly changed the subject. They didn't know that the purpose of doing what he did was to get them both clean.

Sam was going into Derby in the morning, to get some iron, and wanted to know if Eric would like to accompany him. Eric jumped at the chance; it's not as if there would be bellows to pump. That evening, Eric visited Molly's stable, and made sweet smelling love to her.

It was 5 a.m. on a cold, overcast morning, as he and Sam sat at the front of a four-wheeled dray.

In front, two big plodding shire horses pulled them clear of the village.

This, Eric thought, *was the first time he had ventured out since he arrived, some days before.*

The road was narrow, with plenty of ruts and holes. Sam had no trouble manoeuvring the dray around them, he obviously knew them by heart.

It would take Eric thirty minutes by car from Skelton village to Derby city centre; this trek would take at least two hours, if not more. The landscape of fields and hedgerows seemed empty and barren very few cattle grazed, you had to look hard to find a cluster of sheep.

During the civil war, livestock were taken from the fields to feed the troops and even today folk were still wary of the soldiers.

"At one time, the village were very prosperous," Sam told him, puffing away on his clay pipe, clenched between brown teeth.

The nearer they came to the city, the more conscious they were of the smell.

They came to a stone bridge, this being familiar to Eric. Built in the thirteenth century to span the river Trent and its surrounding marshes, the bridge was just under a mile long and still standing in 2020. Consisting of seventeen supporting arches, it is, to the present day, the longest stone inland bridge in England. It is undersized for modern traffic, scarcely two-lane at several points.

Once across, Eric noticed more roads leading off the main one. Hamlets appeared, scattered here and there; he noticed penned livestock and traffic becoming denser. What puzzled Sam was the amount of carts laden with family and belongings, heading out of the city. He became unusually quiet as they entered the gates. The stalls of the market traders were displaying their goods: coopers, tanners, comb-makers, fish, meat, dairy, bread, all venders shouting at the same time, people bustling and shoving. Sam had difficulty getting past them all. Eventually, they came to a large yard by the side of the river Trent, barges moored alongside.

A tall man approached the dray; Sam jumped down, and they shook hands.

"This be Eric," Sam said. "Help's in't forge, and can help wi' this 'erc loadin' o'iron ."

The man pointed to a pile of pig iron.

"How many?" Eric enquired.

"'bout thirty should do it," Sam replied. "I'll gi' thee a hand."

Loading done, the man took Sam to one side and began whispering. Eric moved a little closer to eavesdrop, and what he managed to hear was, "A plague of sorts is spreading through the country, started in London. They tell us seven thousand died in one week!"

Sam paid for the iron, thanked the man, turned the dray around, and they headed further into the city. Pulling into a tavern yard, both men jumped down. Sam watered the horses, and then produced two nose bags from the dray, filled with oats and bran. He secured them to their muzzles. Satisfied, Sam gestured for Eric to follow him into the tavern by the front entrance. Once seated, Sam ordered ale and mutton stew and, making sure they were not overheard, began to explain the conversation with the iron man.

"That explains why folk are filling the streets wi' traffic, panicking," Sam said. "I rekon us at village will be ok," he said, sounding self-assured, just as the meal arrived.

Unfortunately, Eric knew otherwise. This was the Black Death, carried to England in fleas on the fur of rats in cargo ships. In this year of 1665, very few cities in England escaped the Plague. Cholera was also present, being water borne disease. It spread to outlying villages as people fled. Only the Great fire of London, a year later, went some way to eradicate the killer decease.

After their meal, Sam said he had to get some meat and veg' for Molly and, if Eric should want to take a walk round the shops, would meet him back here in one hour. Outside, they both went in different directions. Eric decided to explore one of many cobbled side streets, and maybe buy Molly a small present with the few coppers he had left.

Walking aimlessly, hands in pockets, Eric took in the sights, smells and the closeness of the houses: here the road and pavements were very narrow, the tops of the windows nearly touching. Gutters were filled with excrement, put there by house dwellers throwing out the contents of their chamber pots. A Tudor style bay-fronted window caught Eric's eye, filled with books, cartoon drawings, and large, yellowish newspapers. As Eric pushed the door open, a bell tinkled above. An elderly, white haired man eagerly approached, stooping slightly.

"Can I be of service, young man?" he said, wringing his hands together.

"No thanks, just looking," Eric replied.

Persistently, the man showed Eric a book.

"Just come in," he said. "You look like a man of learning, but then again most are that enter these premises."

The book was by Daniel Defoe, it was 'Robinson Crusoe'.

If only he could take this back with him, he would make a killing on eBay. Eric put down the book, and purchased one of the old yellow newspapers. He doubted whether Molly or Sam could read, but it would come in handy for wiping his arse, back at the forge.

Outside, grey clouds began to appear, threatening rain. No sooner had he left the shop, a fine drizzle began, and Eric knew that within minutes, the affluent packed in the gutters, would become a mass of running filth. Crossing the road, Eric bartered with a woman over a red silk ribbon, paid and stuffed it into his breeches.

Not wanting to venture far from the tavern, he slipped into a side street. Here, the cobbled street and pavements seemed narrower, the shops and houses virtually touching each other at the top windows. To Eric they seemed to be very crooked in structure.

"Hey mister," a woman stopped him by placing a hand on his shoulder. "Like to put your hand up my skirt and have a good feel? A couple o' coppers is all – or we could go somewhere and have a fuck for sixpence. Yo mighten be dead the morrow, what wi' this 'ere plague - what yer say, me lad?"

Eric was shocked.

"No thanks," he spluttered.

"Suit tha sen'." With that, she squatted over the gutter and pissed.

Eric began walking back now in the direction of the tavern, a little shocked by that experience, but it was an everyday occurrence in this period, and he was living it. Sam was waiting for him.

"I've not long since put food stuff in't cart," he said. "We best be off, afore traffic clogs up this 'ere stinkin' city wi' folk who thinks tha knows best than to stay and get this 'ere disease."

Horses watered, fed and already hitched up to the dray, Sam and Eric climbed aboard. The drizzle was light, but the kind that drenched you quicker than driving rain. With blankets around their shoulders and a canvas sheet over both heads, they were ready to go. A click of Sam's tongue, and the big horses began to pull the dray. It was now much heavier than before.

It was late in the evening when they arrived back at the forge. Sam and Eric unloaded the iron quickly, as the rain was now pelting down. Sam dried off the horses once he got them in their stalls, and gave each a hay net to munch on. . The conversation over dinner was the Plague. Sam was trying to explain to Molly the day's happenings, adding a bit here and a bit there, but making it in the least disturbing. Molly seemed more disturbed than her dad.

"What will we do if it reaches here?"

She looked to Eric for the answer. Without sounding too knowledgeable on the subject, Eric explained the importance of hygiene, and sanitary conditions in the back yard, and stressed that the Plague would spread to outlying areas, on rats living off filth, and on the people running from the cities. Before Sam and Molly could challenge him, Eric said he'd heard it said in the city.

"I will make a start on moving the privy in the morning, tidy up like," he said. "It's the least I can do for your hospitality."

Eric pumped the bellows for the best part of the morning, not relishing the next task ahead, when Sam would release him just before lunch. Armed with two buckets of lime and a shovel over his shoulder, Eric set off for the shit pasture, hell in itself. No matter where Eric found himself in time, he would inevitably find himself up to his knees in heavy pungent shit. It was common knowledge to Eric that the problem was where to put excrement and waste in these centuries.

81

It is well documented that the graveyards were full to overflowing in the cities, the gutters running with waste thrown from upstairs windows of houses. In the country you could dig a hole, in the towns and cities it was a different matter. Some ladies would cram it in a large chest in their boudoir before entertaining their men friends. Floorboards would be taken up and the shit thrown underneath. In one instance, a gentleman had been holding a dinner party and, during the meal, the floor collapsed, and most of the guests were drowned in the host's shit.

However, people did survive through the ignorance of sanitation, people like Molly and Sam, good people who knew no different.

I hope by being here, I can help them in some way.

Putting away his thoughts, Eric arrived at the privy, relieved himself of the heavy buckets and set out to find a suitable spot for the new hole. Not too far away from the forge, and not so close to the stream, Eric began digging his selected spot, making sure it was deep enough for Sam and Molly's needs, for a month at least. Tipping over the flimsy wooden structure, dragged it clear of the now overflowing pile, and finally managed to centralize it over the new hole, sprinkling a handful of lime in the bottom, was satisfied with the outcome. He drew the yellow newspaper from his pocket, to be pierced on an existing nail.

Eric dusted down other existing old piles of shit with lime; it gave them the appearance of white mole hills. He then placed a bucket of lime in the privy. Removing his clothes, Eric waded into the stream, and began to wash as best he could. It was a dry, clear day. Not being able to dry off, he put his clothes back on his wet body again. Turning about startled, he found Sam was watching him.

"By 'eck, Eric lad, thar smells grand up ere!"

Eric, pleased with the remark, showed Sam the privy.

"Just remember, Sam, that every time you use the privy, sprinkle a little lime over the top, and don't let it overflow.

"Ee and thar's got paper too, luxury fur our Moll and no messin."

Eric had decided, whilst working at the privy, he would leave the forge. The longer he stayed, the more difficult it would be to leave Sam and lovely Molly. Also, he knew that time would be racing forward back home, and that it may be difficult to explain his absence. He joined Molly that evening in the tavern; they shared gossip over tankards of ale, and also overheard local gossip from a couple of travellers. Apparently the Plague was spreading wildly and killing thousands. The King had fled London, taking refuge in Salisbury. What a time to tell Molly he was leaving! He told her after breakfast, reassuring her that he would be back. Lying again.

Later that evening, he told Sam much the same as he told Molly. Sam was disappointed as much as Molly, but stressing the need to better himself, Eric said that he would venture back towards Lichfield, and maybe find that bloody horse. Snuggling up to Molly in her stall that night, he gave her the silk ribbon.

"Just a little something to remind you of me," Eric said.

"I will always think of my virgin, and the lovely way you talk," Molly answered. Their lovemaking was more ardent this last time, either because she was a good teacher, or because he was getting better at it. He lay with Molly, totally spent.

Breakfast finished, Eric stood saying his goodbyes to them both, Molly pushed a silver button into his hand.

"This is the top one from my blouse, stops me tits from falling out," she said, laughing and winking at the same time.

Eric's parting words were stressed again: use the contraption often, boil all the water, and move the privy often – and don't forget the lime.

Passing the church, he looked into the graveyard. The stench was stronger here, and he tried not to think about why. Walking across the field, he made sure he had the tamper in his pocket. Alongside of it was the button. He remembered from before that he couldn't take items back, only the ones he came through with.

Eric picked a spot in the field, and buried the button; he would find it again with his machine. He reached the exact departure point, lay down, squeezed the tamper in his hand, took one last intake of the foul air of the sixteenth century, rubbed the metal between his fingers, closed his eyes and prayed.

He was back in the tunnel, checked that his bag was safe, and his detector. With impulse Eric snatched up the bag and machine, and made his way out, lucky for Eric it was daylight – blue skies, but cold. Finding the spot he buried the button, he began frantically searching, listening for that signal from his machine.

Maybe I misjudged the spot, he thought. *It's only ten minutes since I last buried it! Hang on, you stupid sod,* Eric's mind started working overtime. *It's been in the ground for centuries! Of course, it might have been dug up by a plough, and it has layers on layers of soil on top.*

He began swinging the metal detector in earnest – then he heard a faint signal.

Heart thumping, he began to take out the soil, which was hard work as he had no spade with him, having left it at home. Putting the detector over the hole again, the signal was stronger.

Not far now!

Taking more soil out, Eric tried the detector again and found no signal at all. Thinking it must be in the discarded soil, he sifted it between fingers and found a hard, round, discoloured object.

It has to be Molly's button! He thought, excitedly, putting it safely in his pocket.

He made his way to the main road.

Eric made a call from the nearest phone booth for a taxi. Twenty minutes later, he was in the city centre, hungry, thirsty and in dire need of a bath. Putting his belongings between his feet, Eric sat on a small wall outside of a church and began to devour a bag of chips and a coke. Even the smell of hot chips could not disguise his body odour.

I have to find a Bed and Breakfast soon, Eric thought to himself.

Selecting one from yellow pages, he began making his way to the address, which was just on the fringes of the centre. The landlady was pleasant, even though she was sniffing the air, and debating whether or not to let the room to Eric when explaining the breakfast. A modest room, soft bed and above all, a bath – it was perfect. After a good soak and change of clothes, he was hungry again; a mixed grill was on his mind.

Friday night in Derby was like any Friday night in most cities: night clubs, pub crawls, cinema goers, girls and blokes drunk and vomiting on the pavement.

Been there, done that – not tonight, thought Eric. *Now where is that restaurant?*

Lying down on top of the bed, hands behind his head, Eric took stock of the past few months. He already missed Molly and Sam. Would he have stayed with them longer, given the choice?

Maybe not, he decided. With his luck, he may well have caught the plague and died.

Had Molly and her dad survived? He would never know. He hoped they had.

After a full breakfast and that long needed good cup of tea or two, he left the house and made a call to his parents.

"Sorry for not calling sooner," Eric lied, "but I just cannot get leave yet. You will get a card from me posted in Derby – a bloke employed here with me is going home for Christmas. I will call on you both as soon as I come over, love you lots!"

He hung up. Over a cup of coffee in a café, Eric got to thinking: I really don't want to hang around Derby, and the sooner I go back somewhere the better.

Eric called into a chemist on his way back to the B&B, he purchased vinegar and distilled water, two of many items you could use to clean coins and soiled relics. Filling the sink with a little vinegar, Eric placed the button in the sink; it would take roughly one to two hours for the vinegar to do its job. In the meantime he visited Mr Crapper's invention. Trousers around his ankles, Eric sat down on the loo, which got him to thinking about those awful conditions that people endured in times past. He reached for the soft toilet paper and sighed.

He washed the button off in the distilled water, using his soft toothbrush to make the button gleam back at him. His eyes filled with tears: it was Molly's button.

After almost a year being away, nothing seemed to have changed. His parents were a little older, most probably think he was dead, there was more mass unemployment, the world still argued over nuclear power. Yet, he could change his world just by the rubbing of his fingers. Somehow, he at last had a purpose in a new life.

I am Eric Middleton, he thought, *and, sod you all, I have the ability of a new beginning – or a deadly end.*

CHAPTER FOUR

For Eric, going back in time now seemed the normal thing, the only question was, just how far he could go? Sitting on the bed, he began sifting through his finds tin; so far he had been transported as near as damn it to the period of each relic, give or take fifty or sixty years.

He picked out a metal buckle, now rusty, but clearly one that had come off a shoe, or breeches – maybe a belt. Eric dated it to be between fourteenth and sixteenth century. Putting the buckle aside, he picked up an arrowhead. This he knew for sure was fourteenth century, from his visits to the local finds museum in Derby. In its normal state it would be triangular shaped, razor sharp edges, barbed for penetrating through skin and flesh. He also had a bodkin arrowhead: this was bullet shaped of toughened iron, forged to penetrate tough leather and armour. Both were used by archers in many skirmishes and battles, mainly with the use of the English long bow – a feared weapon, especially by the French in battles such as Agincourt, and the English civil wars. The best longbow men, though, had always been the Welsh, hired to fight against the French.

91

Selecting the barbed arrow head, he returned the remaining relics to the tin and stashed it at the bottom of the bag. Eric had a fair idea of what lay ahead: if he ended up in the mid- or late fourteenth century he could easily be embroiled in a civil skirmish of sorts, and not forgetting the bloody smell... Eric summarised that in order to escape the filth and smells, he would have to go back to the Roman period, if he could manage to go that far back.

Why not? He thought. *It has worked for me this far.*

Buying a Christmas card and posting it to his parents, Eric decided to go back that very morning. Having a full breakfast inside him, washed down with plenty of tea, he settled up his bill with the landlady.

"Thanks very much for putting me up," he said, shaking her hand.

"That's all right me duck," come back anytime you're in Derby.

Eric threw his bag and detector in the back seat of the waiting taxi, gave instructions, and was on his way. It was two weeks till Christmas.

How time flies, Eric laughed to himself at the pun. *Time flies!* He thought to himself.

On passing his house, he mouthed, "Goodbye, mam and dad – look after one another, until I see you both again, God willing."

It was 11.45 a.m. when Eric reached the farmyard, and bitterly cold. He glanced up to see grey clouds threatening rain or snow. He thought it was strange how, so far, he had managed to avoid confronting Bill or his farm hands. It was just as well, seeing as how he was dressed today – not quite the attire for metal detecting.

So far so good, he thought, and trudged on to the hole.

It felt really cold just this short distance underground, more so than up top. He wondered whether it be summer, autumn, winter or spring where he was going.

I hope to God its summer, I'm bloody freezing stood here, he was thinking, as he prepared to get ready. Let's get it over with.

Relic in his hand, back to the wall, he began his all too familiar transformation.

Eric got his wish; he opened his eyes to the warmth and brightness of the sun. He was pleased with the appearance of his attire this time, not at all like the drab clothing of his previous exploits. Good, stout leather ankle boots, green hose, a brown leather jerkin, and a thin, light brown, soft chamois leather jacket with silver buttons. To finish off, he wore a belt and a long pointed dagger. Not quite nobility, more like a squire – or a minstrel, he decided, and laughed.

The first thing that struck Eric was the silence. Apart from a bird shrieking high up.

Probably a lark, he thought. *They are almost extinct, back home.*

"Here we go again," he said out loud, as he trudged across the field towards the church.

It looked the same, but on closer inspection noticed the graveyard was smaller. He was a bit disappointed, further on down the road, to find no forge, tavern or any homesteads of any kind.

Of course they wouldn't be here, he reprimanded himself. *It's roughly one hundred and fifty years between now and then. Come on Eric, you stupid bugger, and start thinking!*

The road meandering towards Derby was not as wide as before; he turned around and faced the road towards Lichfield, and hoped he would find some sort of habitation going that way.

As he reached the church, he found the door ajar. Why would anyone build a church in so isolated an area, he wondered. Entering cautiously, Eric was confronted with semi-darkness and a dead silence; after his eyes adjusted to the gloom inside, he took stock of the interior. Close by on the left side was a stone font, on each side were four rows of pews, and at the front a stone or marble alter with a wooden cross behind. A pulpit rose some two feet off the ground. Stained glass windows of biblical scenes let in very little light, but enough for Eric to see a dark shape stand up in the front pew and make the sign of the cross.

Eric just stood rooted to the spot, as he recognised a woman approaching him.

"You startled me, I thought I was alone in prayers."

"I'm sorry to have given you a fright," he replied, addressing a very attractive young girl.

She smiled at him and walked on by. Eric thought she walked sedately, angel like, and followed her like a smitten puppy. Outside, they both blinked at the brightness of the sun.

"I haven't seen you in church before, or in the village, where do you hail from?" she looked quizzically at Eric, hands in a white, cotton pouched apron, a white cap perched on the back of her head, the ties dangling loose.

As rehearsed in his head, Eric said he'd got a lift from Derby by cart, and walked the last mile, hoping to find work. She pointed down the road towards Lichfield.

My village is two miles that way. You can try there, but I haven't heard of any jobs going."

She headed for the main road, Eric following, eager to get into conversation with her. He cursed under his breath, these bloody thin soled shoes found every stone, and every now and again she would sensibly walk on the verge, as if she knew the worst parts of the road. They exchanged names, ages and so forth: her name was Agnes and she was eighteen years old. She worked as a kitchen maid for Sir Roland Moorcroft, at the manor. Eric replied that he also was eighteen – his birthday, he remembered, had occurred whilst he was with Molly and her father on his last memorable trip.

"Do you visit the church often?" he said, making small talk.

"I go when I have the time off from the kitchen," she replied, looking down at the road. "I pray for my brother, and all of Sir Roland's men, that they return home safe and whole from the ever pursuing enemy."

Eric gulped.

Bloody hell, what I have I got myself into now, he wondered? He fingered the arrowhead in his pocket. He went on to tell Agnes the old tale of losing his memory, and at times didn't know one year to the next, desperately trying to get the year and date extracted from her. "You poor boy," she exclaimed, showing sympathy for Eric. "Today is fifteenth of August in the year of our Lord, 1485."

"Thanks for that, Agnes, but I do know – it's only now and then I get lapses of memory," he assured her, trying not to sound utterly stupid.

Those two miles seemed endless to Eric, as they came to the outskirts of a village. People were working in the fields, sheep and cattle penned in pastures, thatched crude houses scattered here and there.

"That's Moorcroft manor," Agnes pointed out.

Trees lined a side road leading up to the impressive building. From where he stood, Eric could make out a barn-like structure attached to the side; an archway led to an inner courtyard.

"Sir Roland is a gentleman, but easy to talk to," Agnes explained, as they entered the cobbled yard.

A plump red faced woman blocked the doorway to – presumably – the kitchen, hands covered in flour and crossed over an ample bosom.

"I expected you an hour ago," she said. "I know it's your day off, but we have visitors calling on his master, and he's calling for refreshments. Be an angel, Agnes, and take this prepared tray through to them would yer, I don't know where Beatrice or that scatterbrain Maud is – hiding, no doubt."

Leaving no time for introductions, Agnes picked up the tray on the table and was gone, not even washing her hands or shaking out her dusty skirts.

"Who be you then? Agnes's new boyfriend? She kept that quiet!"

Again he went through his tale to this apparently friendly woman, eagerly taking in the surroundings of the kitchen. An inglenook fireplace was set into one wall, complete with a roasting spit. There was a rough table with chairs and a long slab of stone or marble, running the length of one wall. It was piled high with all manner of food stuffs. Next to this, was a dresser of pots and pans, plates, mugs – in Eric's mind, clutter, as his mam would say. "I hope he can find you a job of sorts, Eric me lad – oh, and me name's Alice. I'm the cook, as you can see, and me better half is Cedric. Bless him, he is Sir Roland's page."

Agnes came rushing into the kitchen with flushed cheeks, her long cap ties swinging from left to right.

"Whatever is amiss gal?" Alice enquired, looking up from her task of rolling pastry.

"Well, I overheard Sir Roland and those men at arms talking about defending a strip of land close by," said Agnes. "I wasn't eves dropping, they was talking so loud," she said, hurriedly. "Too many skirmishes of late for me," Alice said, sadly. "This war is taking too many young lives."

Agnes interrupted Alice, "Oh! Before I forget, Sir Roland will see you when his guests have left. He says he needs all the men he can muster."

Eric gulped and thanked Agnes.

Those bloody relics, it feels like I am being condemned! Eric cursed to himself.

After bread and cheese, and that dreadful low ale, Agnes was eager to show him outside. A time worn water pump was in the middle of the courtyard, flanked by stables and open-fronted workshops, Five shire horses were tethered to rings set in the wall, stamping big, plated feet, their iron shoes creating sparks on the cobbled stones. The way they were saddled and harnessed told Eric that they were war horses. They entered the stables.

"Baldwin, this is Eric," Agnes said, introducing him to a young lad of roughly twelve years old. Even though he was standing on a box, he was having difficulty grooming the back of a horse similar to those outside.

"There were two of us doing these bloody clodhoppers," he complained. "Arthur went on the last skirmish with Sir Roland and never came back, got an arrow in his neck. The master buried him on the battle site – he were an archer. A good 'un and all."

Agnes made the sign of the cross at Baldwin's story.

Pulling Eric out of the stables, she led him across the yard to one of the outbuildings. These were all open fronted, what seemed to Eric to be workshops. A middle aged man was eyeing up an arrow shaft, one eye closed, twirling it in his fingers.

"That'll do nicely," he said to no one in particular. He was obviously very skilled in his work as a Fletcher. "Can't stop to chat now, gal. His lordship wants as many as I can do on me own, been at it since daybreak. I've done two hundred – look, me fingers are raw, and I'm running out of duck feathers and ash saplings – and yew for the long bows. Still, you never seem to make enough, even though you nip out and retrieve the good 'uns, if there be a standoff, but you lose a lot."

He said all of this without looking up, but when he did, he nodded.

"Name's Walter, who are you then?" he asked, looking at Eric with a one-eyed squint.

"This is Eric," Agnes spoke up. "Come to join us."

"I hope he comes to gi' me a hand then," joked Walter.

The next workshop was the forge; Agnes made the introductions amid the noise of hammers on iron. Horace was shaping points on a long lance. Beside him, stacked against a wall, was an array of weapons, all looking heavy and menacing: double headed axes, single ones, swords (short and long handled), maces and flails. Eric was intrigued as to how heavy the swords were, having seen Richard Todd and Errol Flynn swashbuckling in films such as 'Knights of the Round Table,' and 'Robin Hood'. He selected a broadsword and was surprised how light it was, holding it in both hands.

'So, you are a swordsman then,' Horace observed, watching him select the broadsword.

"Not really," Eric confessed. "I'm a cleric, the only thing I wield is a quill," both Agnes and Horace laughed at his wit.

Horace then began to explain the use of various weapons.

"That sword is for close quarter combat on horse, or on foot," he said, pointing at the broadsword. "The long sword is for cutting, slicing and thrusting, and you have the use of the pommel and cross guard as well."

The heaviest implement handed to him was the Flail, a ball and chain – the ball was covered in sharp spikes and fastened to a long chain with an equally long handle. To Eric, it was like having a history lesson in death. He wondered at Agnes and Horace, both of them living day to day, maybe witnessing the effects of these destructive weapons.

I guess if I intend to stay here, I most likely will witness it first-hand, too, he reflected.

Returning to the kitchen, he asked Agnes, "Why is there no help for Walter, Baldwin and Arthur?"

"We did have, but they ventured out with Sir Roland. Many did not return – either they were

103

killed, or just ran off from the field of battle. Skilled men like Walter and Horace stayed here," Agnes explained, with sadness to her voice. "We have more men and women, but they are working in the fields at this moment we speak. My brothers, Conrad and Badric, are toiling out there. Moorcroft is a large estate, compared with some hereabouts."

The men at arms entered the yard. Just as they reached the kitchen door, Eric observed more clearly their mode of dress: all wore chainmail surcoats; each one wore the same livery of Sir Roland's coat of arms over the top, chainmail covering their head and neck, clearly not full armour, daggers and swords dangling from waists. They each used a two-step mounting block in order to mount their huge horses. Once outside the cobbled yard, they spurred them into a canter, churning up clouds of dust that would certainly give them away to the enemy.

Was this really happening to me? Eric wondered. It all felt a bit surreal. This was not quite like other times, with young Tom going off to Portugal, Molly and Sam. *Dear Molly.*

This was more real, more dangerous, and this was only the beginning. Eric's thoughts were interrupted by women's laughter coming from within the kitchen. Two more members of staff, along with Alice, seemed to be sharing a joke.

Was it at my expense? He wondered.

"I'm Beatrice and this is Maud, we're parlour maids to the man himself, and single – or are you taken by our Agnes?" Beatrice giggled.

Eric blushed to his toes, being uncomfortable in the presence of so many women.

"Stop teasing," Agnes said. "I'm just showing Eric around, that's all."

"We believe you, don't we girls?" Beatrice turned to say it to Maud and Alice. "Ho, and by the way, Sir Roland is asking for the young man, now that his guests have gone."

Eric was glad to exit the kitchen with Agnes and avoid more questions from the women. Obviously, his attire was in-keeping with the day, or Beatrice would be the first to comment.

They entered a large, narrow hall. In the centre was a fire place; on each side, trestle tables lined the hall. Eric glanced up: oak beams spanned the roof with thatch above, a hole in the centre to allow the smoke to escape. The floor was of flagstones, yet was covered with rushes; wall sconces were installed at intervals along the walls, where reed torches jutted out.

"Is this were Sir Roland entertained his guests?" Eric asked.

"No, this is our communal dining room," Agnes explained. "Sir Roland had refreshments in his study so he could talk private, like."

Agnes pointed out several guest bedrooms as they passed along a narrow corridor. Finally arriving at a rough oak door, Agnes knocked heavily on a panel.

"Enter," a deep, man's voice echoed.

Eric followed Agnes like a child being taken to the headmaster; they entered a bedchamber, separated by a large fabricated screen with a door, she again knocked more gently and went through.

"Ha, Agnes my dear. Thought it was Beatrice, come to collect these dishes."

"This is Eric, sir," she announced, and began to pile up the remnants of lunch on the tray. "I will take leave of myself sir, and leave you with Eric."

They were in a makeshift study, with table and chairs, the table littered with maps. Tapestry covered most of the walls. Sir Roland was seated, but stood as Eric entered. He was in his forties and tall, with broad shoulders. His hair was centre-parted and rested on his shoulders – it was black, as was his moustache and goatee type beard. His dress was like the gentlemen that had left earlier.

"Well my lad, Agnes tells me your from Derby, and seeking work. To be honest with you, Eric, I don't have the need of a cleric, but I do need men to fight for the King," he said. "We're getting a bit thin on the ground, of late. We have news that an army of Henry's is gathering some miles north of here, and intends to engage with our King in battle somewhere close by. The King has left Leicester and should be here in a few days' time.

"How much do you know of this civil war Eric – seeing as how you're just a cleric? No offence."

"Well, sir, sitting at a desk all day, head down, quill in hand, I only get snippets. It's a dreadful time for us all, sir."

"You seem to be an intelligent young man, so I will tell you the situation we find ourselves in," said Sir Roland, beckoning him forward. "

King Richard has no standing army. He relies on his lords, such as myself, and the fe'alty they hold over their tenants, to furnish troops for him as best we can. My prestige is measured by the 'fe'alty, meaning my workers or tenants are bound by contract to serve me in battle. They wear my livery, and carry my banner. It's a costly affair, Eric, borne by myself. My men at arms, mercenaries, knights – all have to be paid.

"In return, one hopes the King will reward us at court, but above all, Eric, I and others believe in our King. If you wish to stay with us Eric, I expect in return that you learn the longbow with Walter: you never know when you will be needed in battle."

Eric rose from the chair he was offered earlier, thanked this honourable, devout nobleman, and backed away towards the screen. He felt as if he was in the presence of the Queen, by walking backwards he was showing respect – that's how he felt in this man's company. Outside of the bed chamber, he made his way to the great hall. Here alone, he paused to reflect on the situation he now found himself in.

"Bloody hell," he said under his breath. "I'm only days away from the battle of Bosworth Field, in which King Richard III died – the last English King to die in battle, against Henry VII. To be actually involved in this historic period in time gave Eric the cold shivers. He could, of course, leave now and go back to non-historical Derby, but the thought of that made him colder still.

No, he thought, I have to witness this battle first hand, as best I can. I'll keep out of trouble and try to observe at a distance.

"Well?" Agnes asked, as he stepped into the kitchen, with all those female eyes on him.

"I will be staying for a while," he said. "I'm to help Walter, and in return, he is to show me the use of the longbow."

"Don't look too crestfallen, then," Alice remarked, with a cheeky grin. "We are happy for you, aren't we girls, and Walter is a good man. He will teach you well."

"It's only one hour of the clock to dinner, so if you are going to see Walter, you'd better toddle off," chirped in Agnes.

Eric eagerly left the kitchen to the women, and went in pursuit of his teacher. Outside he recalled the smell of ancient filth from the forge, but it was not so pungent here, maybe due to the fact that the Manor and outlying dwellings were more separated. A big manure heap was outside the stables, added to the smells from the forge and just a hint of human excrement in the air. Horace looked up from his work, and gave Eric a cheerful wave as he passed the forge; the burning coke smell bought Sam to mind.

Walter was cursing as he approached the workshop. He looked squarely at Eric, waiting for this young man to utter something.

"I'm to help you, and in return, you have to teach me archery and the use of the longbow," he told him.

"Is that so?" grunted Walter, carrying on with his tasks, then just as quick looked at Eric.

"Does the master not realize that it takes months and years to be proficient in the bow, let alone building up strength in shoulders and arms? To string a longbow and nock an arrow requires strength, lad. However," he continued, sizing Eric up. "Sir Roland is a good, fair master, so I'll carry out his wishes. We will start on the morrow."

Eric took his seat next to Agnes in the hall for the evening meal. Sir Roland was seated at the head; he led them in prayers and welcomed Eric to the fold. Eric blushed crimson as all eyes were on him; Agnes squeezed his hand in comfort and support. He took in the sight of the food laid out on the table, meats of all kinds, cheese, bread and nuts, but very few vegetables. There were wooden cups for everyone except Sir Roland – his was a pewter tankard. Many jugs of light ale were eagerly passed around by the men.

Agnes wasn't wrong when she said that Moorcroft was a big estate. Eric counted twenty people plus children, and a dozen dogs scrounging for bones. Illumination was from candles placed on the table and the torches set in the wall, giving off waves of smoke that escaped through the hole in the roof.

Eric looked for a knife and fork, but there was none, everyone used the knife they carried to cut slices of meat and stab it to death. He remembered that forks for eating were not invented as such, yet they used pitchforks for hay tossing. Wooden spoons were used for soup and stew.

Whilst eating, and not engaging small talk with Agnes, Eric cast his mind back to the privy in Sam's field, and where the one here was. With all these people it didn't bear thinking about.

One thing's for sure, I will not volunteer to move this one.

Dinner over, Sir Roland thanked everyone with a blessing and left the hall. This signalled the time for families and children to get up and leave first, the remainder gossiped on, and finally they drifted out of the hall.

Conrad and Badric, Agnes's brothers came over to them. They both looked happy and contented with life, considering that they could be killed in a few days' time. In fact, you wouldn't think that most of these people had a battle to contend with, laughing and joking as they were, but then again, this civil war has been going on for many years. It must have felt pretty normal by now.

Agnes embraced them, and within just a few minutes, they were both brought up to date of Eric's appearance in Moorcroft.

"Time we were going," Conrad said, "they will be ringing Vespers any time now."

"Yes, and Lauds will come round all too soon," piped in Badric. Outside, Eric heard a bell chime, not loud, but audible. Agnes seeing his bewildered expression on his face remarked that it was from the Monastery some miles distant, ringing for Vespers.

Time was something that puzzled him. He couldn't think how these people managed until he saw a sun dial in the courtyard. Sir Roland, he had noticed, had a tall, fat candle on his table with notches on the side. Alice no doubt cooked with experience and judgement. A worker labouring in the middle of a field had the sun, knowing it to be midday on the sun reaching its zenith, then judging thereafter.

"Did you have a Monastery near to you, Eric?"

"No," he replied quickly.

"Apparently you are staying with Walter and Horace," she told him. "They will be nice to share with. It's not far – I will walk you there."

Agnes loved talking, she never stopped, which pleased Eric no end since he didn't have to keep lying, just listen. She explained the function of the Monastery in the community. Apart from their religious ministrations, they supplied cheese and the ale to Moorcroft, and of course informed them all of the passing of time. She went on to explain that the monks' prayers were twinned with the peel of the bells, hence: Lauds was at the crack of dawn; Prime was early morning; Terce was mid-morning; SEXT was midday; None was mid-afternoon; Vespers was after dinner – then the one which told them it was bedtime: Compline.

"So just listen for the bells," she said.

He was about to say, "How do the monks know the time?" but he thought he better not go down that road, and kept his mouth shut.

They reached the door to a thatched dwelling with daubed walls, and by the moon's light he noticed the door was ill–fitting. Small hessian sacking covered the windows. It reminded Eric

114

of the three little pigs, how the big bad wolf had huffed and puffed, and blown down the houses made of straw and sticks. There would have been no problem for him, here.

"Well, this is where you sleep," she said coyly. Eric whispered his thanks to Agnes, and kissed her on the cheek.

"Sleep well, Eric – see you on the morrow," she began to walk away.

"Will you be alright walking back on your own?" he called after her.

"I have my knife under my apron," she patted it, and walked away into the night.

Eric pushed open the door, which puckered up the rushes on the earth floor; snoring came in unison from the two men on the floor, both lying on straw filled palliasses. He slowly closed the door and kicked back the rushes, thinking how thoughtful they had been to leave a candle burning and a thin course blanket folded and placed on his bed. The room was sparse, to say the least: a pitcher and bowl stood on a small table in the far corner. There was a fireplace on one wall, two little chairs covered by the discarded clothes of the men, and a candle and flint box on another small table. That was it. Eric took off his outer clothing, using them as his pillow, and blew out the candle.

"Come on, lazy bones!" Walter shouted, gently kicking Eric awake. "Get yourself dressed, there's water in yonder pitcher. I'll be in kitchen."

The water smelled foul as he splashed it on his face; his beard was getting a bit matted, he felt.

I wish I had a change of clothes, Eric thought, as he began scratching. No doubt his tenants had found nice warm places on his body and creases in his clothes in which to reside. The hessian curtains were pulled back from the windows, letting in the meagre light. Dressed, made his way to the Manor, hoping he was on the right track. As Eric got near, he wondered what lay ahead of him.

Agnes was sweet and wholesome, had he done the right thing in kissing her? She hadn't rebuked him – maybe he could get one on the lips next time.

The kitchen was crowded, people snatching leftovers from the previous meal, wrapping morsels in muslin cloths, for lunch, no doubt.

Agnes, on seeing Eric, came to him with warm ale, with just a smidgeon of honey in it.

"Help yourself to what's left on the table," she said.

Eric nodded in thanks, took a piece of hard bread and cheese, and then dipped the bread in honey, as he used to do with Sam and Molly.

"This is the Sabbath," Agnes said, standing close to Eric as others left the kitchen.

"Are you not afraid, Agnes? he asked, as they went outside.

"We have all accepted this civil war for so long now, and with God's help, it will soon be over." She sighed, "Yes, Eric, I am afraid. Afraid of losing my brothers and dear close friends."

Eric hoped he was one of her close friends.

Walter was patiently waiting as Eric approached him, armed with two bows, a quiver of long arrows, and a face that told Eric he was not a happy chap.

"Let's go to yonder field and see what you're made of."

For his age, Walter was sprightly in his walk, and Eric had a job to keep pace with him.

"This is just the spot. You can loose a few shafts in yonder distance – that is if you can string 'em," he smirked.

So began the first lesson.

"This here be the longbow, this 'un is a short bow for close quarters."

The long bow was roughly six feet un-strung, whereas the smaller came to Eric's chest.

"Firstly," Walter went on, "you need to learn the art of bending and stringing both bows. I'll show thee first, so take in what I says and does. Remove your drawstring from your pocket, see, and nock one end of the looped string to the bottom of the bow, make sure it is in the groove of the horn, like so, and put the other end in your mouth. Are you right handed or left?" Walter asked him.

"Right," said Eric, dreading this lesson before it had even started.

"Makes a difference see, for your stance," he moved the bow to his left side. "Cross your left leg over the shaft, like so, and put your right foot at the base of the bow to stop it from sliding. Use your left hand to pull down the top of the shaft towards you, it will quiver like a snake, see. Take the string out of your mouth, and set the loop in the groove of the horn. Done!" Walter nodded. "Did you notice, lad, the strength it takes to pull the top down? Now you have a powerful weapon."

Eric tried four or five times to string that bow – it just wanted to keep springing back upright; at the same time, his arms were getting weaker with every pull, until he finally managed it.

"Now string the smaller one," Walter encouraged.

Eric was pleased with himself – he did it first time.

"Right me lad, now to set the weapon," Walter told him. "You will need this." He handed over a thick piece of leather, with a strap and buckle. "Put this on your left wrist – it stops the string from rubbing it raw. The longbow," Walter went on to say, "fires the arrow high into the air, so as it comes down faster, with more force behind it, especially with a barbed steel head on the arrow. The smaller bow is fired direct into the enemy, using a steel bodkin head, for piercing armour."

Eric was shown how to fire both bows; he found the long bow difficult to pull back.

"Kiss the feathers, kiss the feathers!" Walter would shout in his ear.

After some time, Walter left him to practice and headed back to his workshop, but not before telling him, not to forget to collect all the spent arrows.

"I hope this is the first and last time I use these bloody bows," he mused, as he went in search of the arrows.

He sauntered back to the shop around midday, handed in his equipment to Walter, then carried on with the menial tasks he was given. It was whilst sitting at the long table in the kitchen devouring lunch, that Cedric, Alice's husband, blustered into the kitchen, sweating, and out of breath.

"Give me ale, Alice, my dearest! I'm parched, hot, and in need of rest – after I have given the latest news to Sir Roland," he announced. "Tell yer when I come back!" He made for the hall.

"Well," Alice said, "it must be something important, he's been away for days, comes in, and not so much as a 'hello', a kiss, or anything of the kind! Men!"

Walter and Horace began to fidget in their seats; Eric got the impression that they partly knew what was happening. Alice was wringing her hands; Agnes was pulling on her cap ties, her lower lip going white with the biting down of her top teeth. Eric just sat like a lemon, wondering what would happen next. Cedric returned some ten minutes later and sat down. Alice gave him some bread and cheese.

"Well," she asked, "what's happening?"

"I have been instructed by the master not to say anything," said Cedric. "He himself will tell all at the evening meal."

Neither Walter nor Horace badgered Cedric to divulge his news; they simply stood, and made for the door. Eric followed.

"You're best staying here lad," said Walter, seeing him. "I've done all the arrows I can muster."

Alice and Cedric shared a room in the manor, and eagerly left to be alone with each other. Agnes was left to prepare the evening meal; the other two maids shuffled out, giggling as usual.

What was it that amused them all the time? Left alone with Agnes, in this hot stuffy kitchen, Eric was not so inadequate in conversation – with her, he could express himself more.

"Did I do wrong last night, by kissing you?"

Agnes was busy, putting meat in the oven; she turned to face him.

"Of course not! I would have been annoyed if you hadn't," she said. "It is nice to be fancied – when this war is over, maybe we could get together, proper like."

"I would like that, Agnes."

The Hall was a buzz that evening, everyone eagerly awaiting the address by Sir Roland. Finally, he stood; the hall went ghostly silent.

"My friends and workers," he began, "it is with sadness that I have to tell you we will be joining forces with our King in a few days' time. As some of you are aware, Cedric has been away to Leicester on my behalf, gaining information on the King's whereabouts. His Majesty has left the city, and, as I speak, is gathering his army of followers as he ventures here.

"We are to meet at a place called Bosworth, some two days march from here, on Saturday the twenty-second of this month," he continued. "Today is Sunday, our Sabbath, so we will leave on the morrow at midday. Horace will issue weapons and armour, and as usual Walter will supply quivers and barrels of arrows. It just leaves me to thank you all for your support at the manor, and I hope that we all return safely."

Everyone ate in silence; Eric noticed Agnes looking across at her brothers. He could guess what was going on in her mind. He helped her and the rest of the women to clear the hall of food, and return it to the kitchen. Alice was wrapping as much as she could in muslin cloth, placing each item in a wooden crate.

"That should last us for a few days," Alice muttered to herself. "We must burn the candle at both ends and start baking bread now." That remark was addressed to Maud, Beatrice and Agnes. "Come on now, stop looking so shocked and lend a hand," she said. "It's not as if we haven't gone through this before, and as like, this will not be the last time."

Eric was awoken not by Walter's boot, but by the noise of bells peeling and carts trundling by, voices shouting. He dressed, not bothering to wash, and dashed outside, only then realizing that Walter and Horace had already left the house. The courtyard was mayhem, confused people going from cart to cart. It had obviously begun before light. Now it was later in the morning they could see what they had, or had not, stowed aboard. More men at arms had arrived, checking with Cedric that their full armour had been stowed safely in a particular cart. Eric noticed that one cart was piled up with canvas tents and poles, into which Agnes was helping Alice stow food and sacks of bread loafs.

Sir Roland and Cedric were the chief organisers.

"Eric!" a voice bellowed; Sir Roland was gesturing for Eric to approach him. "Since you are new to the fold, I would like you to defend the women as and when – also give a hand on replenishing arrows."

The way he said it, with a comforting hand on his shoulder, Eric could hardly refuse.

It hadn't occurred to Eric that women went to battle until now, and he felt the need to take Agnes into his arms, to hug and kiss her fervently. It was now midmorning; the August sun was warm on his face, as he took Agnes to one side.

"I'm to look after you ladies," he said, "but I guess you don't need a simple clerk like myself, not having been in conflict before."

"Nonsense," Agnes replied. "I, for one, will love your nearness. What better way to get to know each other could there be?"

Eric could think of a better way, but he kept it to himself.

By now, horses were being harnessed to carts. Sir Roland and the men at arms, including Cedric, mounted up. Fifty or so serfs and peasants were wearing iron kettle helmets like sun hats; each had quivers over their shoulders and the long bow they carried like a staff, axes tucked into belts.

It was approaching midday; Sir Roland was handed a long pole with a pennant with his coat of arms fluttering at the top, and the same was handed to a man at arms, displaying the White

Rose of York. Eric was in awe of this fascinating formation. The mounted men were in the lead, followed by archers; the carts taking up the rear, women and children walked beside the carts, followed by a handful of archers to cover the extreme rear. They were off.

Eric was glad that the leading horses, being shires, just plodded along, making the pace more comfortable for the walkers. Little children were placed on carts, if a space could be found. They kept to roads and tracks, but now and again they crossed hard dry pasture land. It was just as well it was August. One hour into the march, the column stopped; word came back that they would rest awhile.

Doing his duty, Eric went from woman to woman and checked if they were alright. Sore feet and thirst were the most common complaints, but there were no serious problems. After refreshment of light ale, they pushed on at the same pace. It seemed to be getting hotter, their feet hurt on the hard packed surface of the roads and their thin leather shoes didn't help.

They rested many times during that afternoon; they were led across a large field and halted. A rider came to inform them that they were to set up camp for the night. It seemed to Eric that every section of the retinue knew how to set up camp efficiently. The horses were tethered to a long line, hay and water given to each. The noble tents were bell shaped, the banners placed at the entrance; the rest were more or less square shaped, with the odd lean-to. Alice set up a kitchen, helped by Agnes, Maud and Beatrice.

"Can I help?" Eric offered his assistance.

"You can fetch some water from that stream," Alice pointed, "and plenty of it."

Conrad sauntered over to us from his section.

"Will these be of use, Alice?" he said, and tossed four rabbits on the ground.

"Good on yer, lad," she beamed. "I were going to do leftovers, but now I'll do rabbit stew instead."

With the stew bubbling in three large cauldrons, the women and children rested in their respective shelters. Eric sought out Agnes, who was chatting with her brothers.

"Thought you would like to take a walk with me before supper," he ventured.

"Alright," she said and came to his side.

"Keep inside the encampment," Badric advised. "Even though we have sentries posted, the bloody red roses might be closer than we think."

They both, in unison, agreed to adhere to Badric's wishes. Out of earshot, Eric said, "Badric is a strange name."

"It means 'the axe ruler'," Agnes laughed, "but he is gentle really."

Eric purposefully wanted to see and digest the entirety of the camp. They walked, Eric asking loads of questions, Agnes eagerly replying. They finally found a spot away from prying eyes, and sat down on the grass.

"Being a clerk, I know nothing of all this," he gestured. "That's why I put so many questions to you."

"I understand Eric, I don't mind in the least," she said. "In fact, I love talking to you."

"Does it worry you, Agnes, that you may not return to Moorcroft, and not have done all the things you wish to do?" he asked.

"Of course it does, but what are we to do? Be ruled by another King, change our ways to suit theirs? The men here think not, Eric, and they fight for what they believe in."

"Would you let me kiss you properly Agnes? Let me hold you tightly? Hug you, make you feel wanted, and not be taken for granted by others?"

"You say wonderful words, Eric," she said, candidly. "I have never met anyone quite like you before. Yes, hold me Eric."

Agnes was soft in his embrace, he tilted up her face and kissed those rosebud, kissable lips. She didn't smell, like Molly had, hers was more of an open air, fresh smell.

Supper was served just before the light failed; they all queued with their wooden bowls. Alice ladled out a portion to each bowl offered, and they ripped a chunk of bread off a loaf; weak ale in jugs was plentiful. With the resources available, Alice made wonderful meals: the chunks of rabbit in the stew was as tender as chicken. As they marched, she would nip off, and return with a bucket full of vegetables, or berries, so dedicated to her work was Alice.

The four women shared a tent. Eric assumed he would be with Walter and Horace like before, but to his astonishment, he was invited to lay his head down next to Agnes. A spare palliasse was laid for him there. After the day's march, people were so tired that they retired soon after their meal.

I'm totally knackered, myself, Eric mused, as he lay next to Agnes. The other three women were snoring soundly, each covered by a blanket.

"Would you like to come under my blanket, Eric?" she whispered softly.

Did she honestly think he would say no? As he slid in beside her, he decided he had obviously misjudged Agnes's devout approach, but it was dark, and she was after all, a young pretty woman with needs like any other.

"You got me to thinking Eric, when we spoke earlier," she whispered. "About doing things we wished, and not fulfilling them because we might not come back. Well, this is one of them Eric. I haven't been de-flowered yet."

"Won't we wake them up?" Eric said.

"A thunderstorm over this tent would not make them blink," Agnes assured him.

He was as tender as he could be with her, considering the narrowness of the palliasse, kissing her passionately and running his hand over her pert breasts, her nipples responding immediately. She wore a thin shift and there was no underwear in this period; he lifted it up to waist level, and then gently put his hand between her legs, and she gave a shudder, instinctively arching her back.

"Thank you Eric," she said, as her breathing began to be normal. "Now I can hold my head up amongst the woman, knowing what pleasure a man can give a woman."

During breakfast, Eric noticed Alice give a cheeky wink to Agnes.

After two days of slow walking, we merged with another band of men. This column was much bigger than ours, more men in light armour, more banners flying, hundreds of archers; Eric could only just make out the nobles talking up at the front before they rode off and halted, two fields away, and set up camp. Sir Roland decided to camp in sight of these new allies. During his many walks of the perimeter, and seeing this sight of fighting men, he wanted desperately to approach the leaders and plead that they withdraw, because they would not win their cause. It was so hard not to shout out.

Cedric brought him out of his trance.

"Hello Eric. I haven't seen much of you of late – the master keeps me by his side, I'm afraid," he said. "My task is to dress him in armour, and also his mounted men."

"Do you take up arms?" Eric enquired, curious.

"No, my job's done when they leave for battle," he said. "I hear you're to replenish the archers. Do it quickly Eric, then get your head down, they shoot volleys, as well you know."

The column began to march again at first light, with the amalgamation of yet more troops appearing en-route. It was now Thursday midday, the sun beat down relentlessly. The people, including Eric were tired, dirty, and in need of a long rest. He wondered how much further it was to Bosworth. By car, it would have taken forty-five minutes. He reflected that transport was something that the modern world took greatly for granted.

The column stopped, then went forward a dozen paces, then stopped again; people began bunching up.

"Now what?" was the spoken, irritated question of many in the ranks. Cedric came riding back from the front of the column.

"This is as far as we go for now, Sir Roland wants that we should make camp here," he announced.

All the carts were placed side by side in a corner of a huge field – it looked more like an open plain. Tents were put up, horses cared for. There was ample room for the other column that had joined earlier. Apart from her chores, Agnes never left Eric's side.

"I think this is it, Eric," she said. "From here they will ride and march to battle."

"Unless we have more support, we haven't a hope in hell," Eric said.

"Don't be silly, Eric, the King and his men have yet to come," she told him. "And Cedric says plenty more noblemen and knights will join us."

"I hope he's right," said Eric, pretending he knew nothing of the impending fate of this battle.

He began checking the barrels of arrows, deadly looking barbed ones and bodkins, he remembered Walter's explanation of a good archer: 'he could fire fifteen arrows a minute, given the chance'.

"I wonder how many a quiver holds?" he said to himself. "Looks like I have my work cut out – and at the same time, trying to keep alive. Bloody hell."

It was around mid-afternoon, judging by the slant of the sun, that Eric noticed a huge cloud of dust just off to his left, but further forward than they were. He grabbed Agnes's arm.

"Come on, let's go up front and have a scout around," he said.

"Do you think we should – it could be dangerous? They could be enemy, even," Agnes said, nervously.

Eric didn't give her a reply, just propelled her forward.

The sight that confronted them left Eric spellbound: field after field was crammed with troops, literally hundreds of banners fluttered in the slight August breeze. The sun was bouncing off polished armour, dazzling to the eye. He quickly calculated thousands of men.

"Christ," he said, under his breath, and they moved quickly back to a safe area.

"That has to be King Richard's army," he said, excitedly to Agnes, "and amongst them is the man himself."

Eric hadn't long got those words out when Sir Roland and the other nobles rode away towards the great mass, each one flying their colours.

"Cedric was with them," Agnes noted. "We could ask him questions on his return. Alice must be proud of her man, riding along with the lords and nobles, even though he is just a page. But I wouldn't like it, if it were you," and with that she nuzzled up to Eric.

Later that day, Cedric took his evening meal with the group, and they got to know all that was happening, in between the hugs and kisses he was showering on Alice.

"The King is in place, and required to know our strength," said Cedric. "He estimates our final mass of troops to be in excess of twelve thousand – that's if we are supported by Lord Stanley and his brother, who commands four thousand troops. Sir Roland says the King suspects their loyalty is elsewhere, and could switch at any time, but he is prepared to gamble.

"Lord Northumberland's troops will act in a supportive role," he continued. "Bosworth Field is yonder, less than a mile away. That's where he intends to engage Henry. You, Alice, my dear, and the rest of the women and children are to stay here. With God's grace I will return to you Alice."

This is it then, thought Eric, history coming to life before my eyes – the ending of the house of Plantagenet, and the beginning of the Tudor period. I wonder how Agnes will take to being ruled by a different King or Moorcroft Manor changing hands?

No one got much sleep that night, with the thought of the enemy being so close and the battle only hours away. It left little imagination as to how the married people felt. Cedric joined

Alice for the night, so what with Agnes and me, and Cedric and Alice there was definitely not much sleep in that tent the night.

Friday afternoon on the twenty-first of August, 1485, the men of Moorcroft Manor hitched up the horses to the carts, said their goodbyes, and moved out, Eric among them. He drove the arrow cart, Walter staying behind. They eventually arrived at their destination. Eric noticed the fields around us were soft and bog-like, but managed to follow instructions as to where he should place the cart.

A bell tent was being erected in the field to the left, a large banner was being unfurled, with a white boar in the centre – above it was a crown of gold. As yet, Sir Roland's men were grouped together; Eric just sat on his wagon and observed all that was going on, terrified to say the least. Light was fading.

I could do with Alice's stew inside me right now, he thought. *An army can't fight on an empty stomach – now, where have I heard that saying before?*

Braziers were being lit as far as the eye could see. Eric was getting a bit annoyed, just sitting there, waiting.

Cedric sought him out.

"Come on down lad, and take some warm ale with me."

He led me to one of our braziers; a bowman was heating up ale in a pot, some bowmen were eating bread with theirs. It tasted foul, but it was warm.

"What's happening now?" Eric questioned Cedric, as if he knew all the answers.

"Well, no sighting of Henry as yet – our scouts are poised out there," he pointed to a vast open space, just visible with the fading light. "It could be a long night, Eric. When the bowmen finally line up lad," Cedric went on to say, "only fill our bowmen's quivers up, even if other lines shout for replenishing – they have a boy to fill them up, just like you."

He thanked Cedric for the ale and advice and began to walk back to his cart. He was right about it being a long night. Eric wedged himself between the barrels, pulled the canvas covering over him, but it was rest, not sleep, he got: he was listening for that shout of "Stand to arms!"

It came just before the dawn.

He jumped down, flustered and bewildered, walked over to the bowmen, who were stringing their bows.

"Get them barrels here, close by," one shouted to Eric.

He rushed back and began carrying the barrels from the cart to the nearest man. They were small and no weight at all. The bowmen were in a line, like dominoes; not just Roland's men, but what seemed like thousands, as far as the eye could see – all facing this great span of open waste ground. Eric began placing a handful of arrows in each man's quiver, slung on his back. He was sweating, with heat or fright, he didn't know; all he kept thinking of was 'This arrow I have given to this man will, kill another, or maybe a horse.'

Each man had a shield at his side, and each section had a leader, who stood in front. Then a spectacular thing happened: the middle of the mass of bowmen opened up and hundreds of horses cantered through. The King was in front

139

in full armour, as were all the knights, men at arms, and nobles. All carried shields bearing their individual coat of arms, all carried swords – some sheathed, some out – axes, pole-axes bristled along the line. Pennants fluttered in the summer breeze, the white boar announcing the King's presence.

How can they see, let alone fight, with just slits in many of the helmets? Eric wondered.

Horses, too, were in armour: chest plates, and face armour. Behind them came thousands of infantry, all armed with various weapons.

Then, in the distance, across the waste ground, Eric spotted the enemy. He could just make out a dark mass, then the longer he looked, the closer they seemed to be.

King Richard was ready, so it seemed, yet he watched Henry forming up his troops.

Could that have been what sealed his fate? Eric waited with bated breath, seeing history unfold. The section leaders ordered arrows to be placed nocked; he noticed a mounted man in front raise his lance – when he was certain the enemy were in striking distance, he dropped his arm. A deafening whistle pierced Eric's ears; the sky

140

was darkened by thousands of arrows, climbing over the heads of Richard's men, it seemed an age before they began their descent onto the enemy.

He couldn't tell what carnage was caused at this distance, but the whistling began again, getting louder – these arrows were destined for Richard's men, Eric among them. Shields were raised over heads, Eric dove under the cart. By the time he emerged, the archers were firing again. He began to fill the quivers at a fast pace, stepping over fallen men and trying not to think to hard about their dead, staring eyes. The remaining archers were now firing at a faster pace, and at one point arrows were crossing each other in flight.

"Bugger this for a lark!" Eric said; he took a shield from a dead man and ran for the cover of the cart. A lull in whistling gave Eric the chance to emerge, to see the devastating effect of those arrows. The line of archers had been thinned considerably, some horses were down with arrows sticking from their rump or shoulders, desperately trying to get up. Those riders that had not been crushed were gathering composure and their weapons; at the

141

same time advancing towards each other at a very slow pace. He made a few more attempts at filling quivers, and then he saw that the enemy were close to Richard. The archers discarded their bows, took up their axes and charged across the plain.

At this point, Eric felt alone, and utterly useless, looking across at the bloody battle taking place before him: thousands of men battering each other to death. He had seen Sam and Horace strike the anvil countless times, shaping a piece of metal to perfection. In this case, each man was trying to deform the metal, to get to the human being inside and smash it to a pulp.

It was at this time in his travels that Eric wished he could change time and occurrences, but he knew that the events unfolding here had already happened. Eric witnessed what he wanted to, and knew what the outcome would be.

"I wonder if Sir Roland, Conrad, Horace, and Badric made it – and what of Cedric?" he wondered aloud. "He should be around here somewhere, shouldn't he?"

The cart took a few hits; he wriggled them free, and then snapped them over his knee. It was at this point that he noticed the dreadful smell, a mixture of blood and excrement – the latter happening as the bowels opened uncontrollably in sheer terror, or immediately following death. The noise was still deafening.

I must get away from this carnage – but how?

Eric was harnessing the horse to the cart when Cedric appeared.

"Come on lad, we need to get this cart moving forward for the injured, quickly like" he said.

Eric led the horse by the reins, following Cedric to the outer fringes of the battle; the fighting seemed to have stopped, but it was difficult at this range to see for sure. What was sure was that bodies and horses littered the area; horses kicking, trying desperately to get up, the wounded men crawling over one another, the ground soaked in so much blood.

"We only take our own, Eric," Cedric told him, grimly. "Sounds heartless, I know, but they will mop up their own in good time. Our wounded will try and retreat to our first line, theirs to yonder."

"Is it not dangerous for us to wander around?" Eric nervously asked.

"We are too far away, lad."

They had been on the verge of going back when Conrad approached them, limping badly, holding up a lifeless Badric. Both of them were covered from head to foot in blood.

"Where are you wounded?" Cedric inquired of Conrad.

"Got a bloody sword thrust in't thigh," he grimaced. "I saw Badric go down, not sure what his injuries are, only know he's alive. Don't gawp Eric, most of this blood is from others," he said. "Best we leave now, this leg is bloody killing me."

As they staggered back to the cart, an almighty cheer went up from the centre of the waste ground; it reminded Eric of a goal scored at a premier football match.

"We were outnumbered," coughed Conrad. "Badly. Richard didn't get his support from Lord Stanley. The bastard turned sides."

"God help our survivors down there, if they don't raise their swords in alliance with Henry, another slaughter will occur," sighed Cedric.

They stopped frequently on the return to the women, mainly to see to the men's injuries; a wooden cart and rutted roads didn't help. Women and children gathered around the cart as it trundled into camp. Gingerly, the injured, including many more of Roland's men picked up on the way, were placed onto beds. The women fussed and treated them as best they could. Agnes was alarmed to see that Eric was covered in blood.

"Don't fret Agnes, it's not mine." Relieved, Agnes then went over to her badly injured brothers.

"We lost the war then?"

"Afraid so," he said. "Cedric suggests we leave as soon as possible, only take the tents needed for us – the rest can stay, just in case some of our men make it back here."

By midday, they were a small convoy heading back to Moorcroft. There were no banners flying this time, just a sombre defeated column of quiet people. Sir Roland was nowhere to be found. He might have survived, but Cedric feared the worst.

Eric stayed at the manor for a couple of days: Conrad's leg was healing, Badric regained consciousness after being bludgeoned on the head and Cedric took the role as steward of Moorcroft in the absence of his master. Walter looked much older than he had before the battle, and was often bored, as no arrows were needed. He also missed Horace and his master. Young Baldwin had no horses to tend to, so he was given the task of moving the smelly privy.

Eric felt that he had had a narrow escape on that score. The wives of men lost were taken to work in the fields, to keep their minds off their lost loves. Eric helped Cedric stash away Sir Roland's valuables, and destroy all paper work. King Henry's men would be arriving soon to commandeer Moorcroft, and they would have no choice but to go along with their new regime. Agnes and Eric spent those nights together in a guest room – they had a lot to catch up with.

Eric had come through with the arrow head, had seen what he wanted to and had a blissful time with Agnes, but it was time to go.

The opportunity came when Agnes wished to go to church, saying she wanted to pray for the dead, and pray for more of Moorcroft's men to return – in particular, Sir Roland. They left in the morning, the walk seeming longer this time than before. Most of the conversation was of a sombre nature. He didn't relish what he soon would be doing to sweet Agnes. It was not as if he could kiss her and say 'See you soon, love!'

He could easily have done that, but he felt it would be too cruel – her waiting for a reunion that would never happen. It would be best to just disappear.

Agnes entered the church first; Eric made an excuse that he needed to relieve himself first, and then ran to the departure point.

He lay down in the tall grass with the relic in his hand. He closed his eyes, rubbed the arrowhead, and – as they say – that's history.

CHAPTER FIVE

Eric got to thinking, as he sat on the same bed as before, that the landlady had difficulty in recognising him after being away for so long.

His thoughts of course were of Agnes, and the deceitful way he had left, but that's what this time travelling was about. You got involved with people's lives, like it or not. The only answer to this would be to remain there for good.

Would I like to do that? he asked himself. *The answer, at this moment in time, is 'no',* although there could be a small possibility that one or two little Middletons had been running around in the sixteenth and fourteenth centuries. He would never know.

Standing at the wash basin shaving, Eric studied himself in the mirror. His hair was longer, now reaching his shoulders; there were no extra lines on his face that he was aware of, yet he felt older somehow. His landlady looked older, and his parents sounded considerably older on the phone.

If I decide to go back, there's a chance that I may never see them again, but what do I do? The thought really pulled at Erics heart strings.

His relic tin contained more of the run of the mill objects. Putting aside the penny, the tamper and arrowhead, he took out one item that would put him in the thirteenth century – was a silver sixpence coin. The size of a farthing, worn nearly smooth by constant handling, he could just make out a king's head, and on the obverse a cross. Eric looked it up in his monthly *Treasure Hunting* magazine. It appeared to be that of King John or King Henry, and the cross was not biblical as he first thought, but was so that the coin could be cut into four quarters for bargaining purposes. It was dated at around 1216.

He had dug it up near the church, and as the church was built around the twelfth or thirteenth centuries the find gave Eric a buzz. It was one of his older finds of coins. Over a period of several days, Eric toyed with the idea of going back with the coin.

If I do go back, he thought to himself, it will be the very last time. There's not much left in the tin worth considering.

For some unfathomable reason, Eric had a feeling of not belonging in 2020, yet when he was in the past he seemed to have more confidence in himself. The people seemed friendlier, even though life was a struggle for them – they were happier in themselves.

Strange isn't it, he mused, all those centuries behind us and we today are no better, what with fighting all over the globe, mass unemployment, house shortages, overpopulation, large-scale poverty, it just goes on and on. At least back there, what you don't have you don't miss.

Eric got himself so depressed thinking about all this that he couldn't wait to go back.

He made one final telephone call to his parents, after all, this may be the last time he sees or speaks to them.

The silver penny clutched in his hand, Eric opened his eyes to yet another warm day. Strangely, he was dressed as before, obviously there was not much of a change in clothes from this period to the next. Eric stood and took in his surroundings, something was wrong – but what? The field looked the same, the church –

Eric froze. The church, that's what was missing! The church steeple in the distance, his one and only visual guide, was absent.

As he walked in the direction of the missing church, he noticed people milling around what would one day be the church site. On closer inspection it was all too clear: these were workers, the builders of his church. The foundations were laid: the church stood three layers high, made of blocks of large stone. A Norman style doorway was being built, two men were using an a-frame to lift and place the heavy, dressed stone.

He walked around, unsure whether he would be accosted at any minute. He definitely felt overdressed compared to these people. He happened upon a young lad, no more than sixteen, carving a date in a huge stone with chisel and mallet. The date was 1215, and the scroll work around it was exquisite.

"Hello sir," he said, as Eric's shadow fell over him. "Have you come to scrutinise my work?"

"Err no," Eric faltered for words, and also at being complimented by the word, 'sir.' The level of respect he was receiving from this young lad completely threw him. "Just passing through," he managed to say.

They were joined by a tall, fit looking man. He had the look of a man in charge.

"Can I help you, sir? Name's Thomas, I'm the master stonemason."

Eric went through his story yet again.

"Well' it's the local Monastery that's funding this build," Thomas said. "You need to speak to father Gilbert, the Prior – he should be visiting us soon. We are taking our midday meal shortly, you are most welcome to join us."

Eric was overwhelmed by the generosity and friendliness of these poor people, to offer a complete stranger food – this is something that would not happen back home. It was Anthony, the young, gifted carver, who shared his meagre food with him, sitting on a slab of stone. Eric looked at Anthony's hands, as he forced a chunk of bread in his mouth, they were scared from stone chips, fresh blood ran from old scabs. Anthony noticed him looking.

"Sharp as flint, some of these chips are," he said. "No sooner they heal, a flying piece of stone will hit the same bloody place."

"How long have you been working here? Eric said.

"From the first stone laid, some months back – and by the rate they are being laid, some years to come," he answered with a grin.

With the workforce now all seated at various intervals around the church site, Eric could see where Anthony's remark referring to it taking years came from. He counted just eight people, nine with the lad sitting next to him; among them, he noticed a girl.

A monk entered the site, his bare legs astride a small horse, and sandals on his feet. Thomas approached the visitor, and helped him dismount. He appeared to be quite small in stature. After talking for a few minutes, they both came over.

"Eric, is it not?" the small figure addressed him. "Thomas has informed me you are seeking work."

"Very well, come to the monastery with the others this evening, and we can discuss it further."

That was the prior's last word, as he turned and walked away with Thomas.

"You'll like him – the prior, I mean – if he gives you work," Anthony told him. "Been good to me he has, took me in when I were little, learned me letters and stuff."

Anthony also explained that his parents died of a disease; they were serfs of the monastery.

"Well, suppose I better get back to me work," he said and sauntered off, leaving Eric bewildered as what to do next.

He stared at the building, and tried to imagine it built. When he and Agnes had been inside he didn't take much notice, now he wished he had.

The stones they were using looked like Derbyshire stone, the same as his house was built of, but on a larger scale. Two men lifted each stone easily from the ground, placing it on top of the wall and using very little mortar, as the stone was heavy in itself. This, he noticed was happening at intervals around the circumference of the build. The Prior and Thomas, he suspected, were consulting with each other from sheets of architectural drawings, Thomas pointing to various points of the walls. Eric strolled over to where the girl was working. She glanced up in the throes of her labour.

"You haven't come to work in those clothes have you? Far too grand for this kind of work!" she said. "Look at me – me skirt's supposed to be black, but it's nearly white with this lime dust. Still, it'll wash out. Name's Amy," she said, and proffered a white, grubby hand.

Eric, shook her hand, at the same time taking in her appearance: Amy was more or less dressed like Agnes – a white linen cap tied under her chin, white linen collar, black skirt, white apron. She was astonishingly good looking beneath the smudges of dried mortar. She was mixing lime, sand, and water in a large, cut down water barrel, using a wooden paddle. When the mortar was at the correct texture, she would fill wooden buckets with it; these, in turn, were carried away to various building points by labourers.

"Why are you doing such a heavy task?" Eric asked her.

"Because I can't lift heavy stone, and I don't have skills like Anthony does at carving and cutting stone – or the carpenters. So in order to live and keep my cottage, I chose to mix mortar."

Satisfied with Amy's response, Eric changed the subject and explained his presence here at the site.

Some hours later, after the Prior had left for the Monastery, Thomas called a halt in work. Dark clouds were gathering overhead, threatening rain. Two flat bottomed carts were the transport home, again pulled by big, heavy shires. Within a few minutes, everyone was sitting side by side, feet dangling. Thomas sat up front on the leading cart; the skilled men with their tools in canvas bags slung over one shoulder sat together laughing and joking. Eric found himself sandwiched between Amy and Anthony. They more or less travelled the same route as Eric had walked to the manor with Agnes.

In no time at all, they passed the entrance to the manor, but now it looked just like a large house, no trees lined the roadway to it: it looked very isolated and lonely. Conversation between Amy and Anthony was non-existent during the short journey to the Monastery, mainly due to the creaking of the cart, and the wheel noise on the rutted, hard surface of the road.

With the Monastery in sight, Eric noticed the labourers and craftsmen jumping off the cart and disappearing into various cottages. Obviously they were married men with families. The street here was cobbled, with cottages either side of the street. He noticed that some were shops, their small window shutters lowered by hinges, supported by wooden legs underneath and their goods laid out on display.

This, Eric thought, *was a proper village.*

They approached a high–fronted, walled building. An older looking monk pushed open huge double oak doors; the cart trundled through it into a large courtyard. The doors banged shut behind them and were quickly bolted by the brother porter. Thomas was the first to jump down, followed by the three teenagers. They entered a long hall, trestle tables and benches in the middle. A table at the far end contained a bowl and pitcher, and a neatly stacked pile of towels. A log fire burned at the side of the hall.

Having washed their hands and faces, Eric followed the rest to sit at the end of the table. A wooden spoon and mug were laid for just the four of them. No sooner had they sat down, they were served hot stew, bread, and warm ale by two young boys, both dressed in grey habits. They were obviously novices, because they had normal hair. Eric was famished and picked up his spoon only to be stopped by Thomas.

"Prayers first, lad," he said, and then uttered a short prayer.

Once grace was over, Thomas tore off a chunk of bread, and passed the loaf around. The stew was one of the best Eric had ever tasted on his travels. This was followed by cheese – the ale was almost as sweet as wine.

"When you have had your fill, Eric, I will take you to Prior Gilbert's house," Thomas addressed him.

"I've finished now," Eric said, getting up from the table. Amy and Anthony followed suit.

"I'll be off to me bed, then, see you all in the morning," Anthony remarked, and walked out of the hall.

"I hope all goes well with you Eric, and I see you on the cart in the morrow. "I best be off home, a lot of chores to be done before I can get to me bed," Amy said, leaving the hall the same way they had come in.

It was more of a guided tour, as Thomas led the way to the Prior's house. They passed the Infirmary, the Herbarium, the latrines, the dormitories, guest rooms, church, stables, forge, brewery, bake house – the size of the place was like putting three, massive football stadiums together. Each part of it was like a building in itself, surrounded by a high wall.

Finally, they arrived at the Prior's door. A novice answered Thomas's knock.

"Please come in, the Prior is expecting you," he led them to his study.

"Welcome, Eric. Please sit down – thank you Thomas, there's no need for you to be here, I will see you at the site in the morning," the Prior dismissed Thomas politely. "So, young man," the Prior began. "You are seeking work, and you are a trained cleric I am told?"

"Yes," Eric replied, going through his story yet again.

"Well, Eric, we have brother Enor the bursar, he looks after the accounts and also keeps an eye on the money. His name reminds me of a donkey," the Prior chuckled. "He is small and rotund, and he prefers to ride a donkey rather than a horse. I feel sorry for the donkey. Anyway, he is a good and honest man. We are self-sufficient here Eric, we make our own bread and cakes, wine, ale, cheese, fruit, we also have a blacksmith, an infirmary.

"It is endless, Eric – and do not forget that most of the older brothers here were fighting veterans of the crusades, like myself," he told him. "We can defend ourselves if necessary. This Monastery and land belongs to the Diocese of the Bishop of Derby. He is the head of the region, the Abbot is also in Derby, and I am the head of this monastery.

"We sell our goods at the market in Derby. The proceeds go towards building the church – we very much need this church Eric. Parishioners come to the church here within the monastery. We school the children, but the parish is growing fast. If we had a parish church, we could have our own fairs and markets on the church grounds. It would bring outside people to us, and I don't need to tell you, Eric, what an impact that would have on the parish.

"You probably noticed a manor house on your ride back from the site," he continued. "Well, that belongs to Sir Wilfred Moorcroft.

He lives there with his two sons. All three are soldiers. He governs a garrison near Derby, and he owns all of the land around the monastery, and his serfs tend the fields. Some of the cottages you see are his. If there are any discrepancies within the parish, he is judge and jury, but other than that his involvement with the church is nil.

"I was trained as an architect as a novice, and gained knowledge from many churches I visited in foreign lands during our crusades," he told him. "So between Thomas and myself, we have painstakingly drawn up the plans for the construction of the church. The job I have in mind for you Eric, if you wish to undertake is, to keep stock of building materials, ordering, and security. The latter being important very important. It seems stone has been taken from the site. It is one of the expensive of all the materials.

"You will take over the ledger from Enor. I take it you can ride, and use a weapon?"

"Yes, I am proficient in the bow," boasted Eric. "I would be happy to take the task on."

"Good," said the prior. "You shall take a guest room and all food will be provided here. I'll see that a horse will be provided for you. A silver sixpence every two weeks will be your wages."

The novice led Eric to a clothing store.

"These will be more fitting for day to day work," he said, handing him coarse hose, a shirt, a jerkin and leather knee length boots.

Apart from the black boots, the clothing was all brown in colour. Arms full, and now running across the courtyard as the rain was pelting down, they entered the bursar's room. The prior's description of the man was true to form, except that he didn't mention the monk's squint: one eye moved, the other didn't.

Eric took the ledger from him, explaining his new role, then made a quick dash to the guest room that had been laid out for him. There was a wooden framed bed with a crucifix above, a candle and flint box, a chair, a table with a bowl and ewer of water. That completed Eric's accommodation.

"You take meals in the same room as you had supper in," remarked the novice, they shook hands, and he was gone.

Eric didn't get much sleep. He was woken by chanting and bells at certain intervals. Putting the pillow over his head, plus a spare blanket, didn't work, he kept waiting for the next bout of chanting. The chanting he now was hearing was different, more like a banging.

"Eric! Eric!" Thomas was calling through the door. "Time to wash and have breakfast before work. I'll see you in the hall."

I must have had some sleep, Eric mused, as he washed in ice cold water. He put on his work clothes. With the knife on his belt and his boots on, he was ready to face a new chapter in his life.

Thomas and Anthony were already seated, and looked up as he entered the hall and sat down.

"What time is it?" Eric inquired.

"It's nearly work time replied Anthony."

After breakfast, each was given a little, tied linen bag and a corked pitcher of ale between the three of them. Outside, the night was lifting, enabling Eric to just make out the waiting carts and a groom holding a saddled horse.

"This is your transport, master Eric," he said, giving him the reins.

Eric led the horse over to one of the carts to speak to Amy, who was seated alone.

"I see you have employment then," Amy observed, before he could open his mouth.

"Yes, but I'm sorry I won't be sitting next to you on the journey. I have to ride this old girl," he patted the horse's greying nose. "But I hope to sit with you at lunchtime."

"I'd like that," she said.

With Thomas and Anthony now on board the cart, they moved out of the opened gates, the second cart following behind. Eric waited until they were clear of the monastery, before mounting his horse. He had never ridden before, but he had read about it in stories, this was for real. He put his left foot in the stirrup and heaved himself up and over, at the same time the horse went round in circles; he managed to slip his other foot in the stirrup, and get the horse to face the gates.

His ledger, charcoal and presumably lunch was in the linen bag, safely in one of the saddle bags. One little squeeze of the legs, and the horse responded slowly. Ahead, he saw the carts picking up the men along the way. The weather was dry, but a cold wind hit his face; the warmth from the horse, travelled up his legs. As he passed the Manor, Eric gave a silent kiss to Agnes, who hadn't been born yet.

On reaching the site, they all dispersed to their allotted place of work. The cart drivers unharnessed the horses, and turned them out into an adjacent field. One driver came over to Eric.

"You will find something in one of the carts for you," he said. "The prior insisted you should have them, he said. By the way, your horse is named Beth. She is old, but faithful."

He joined the other driver in labouring tasks. Eric unsaddled Beth, and put her with the others to graze. He took out the ledger from his saddlebag, made his way over to the cart and peered over the side. He was amazed to find three swords, three bows, plus three full quivers, and a bundle of pikestaffs.

The prior wants this church built at all costs it seems, Eric thought. I wonder how many of these men can use a weapon. Would they defend the church at all costs?

Eric noticed Thomas talking to two men, deep into conversation; he walked over to them, but politely stood back until the discussions were at an end.

"Take a cart and cut down strong, thick saplings," he was saying. "We are just about ready to begin erecting the scaffolding."

"I don't wish to intrude," Eric said to Thomas, as a gap appeared in the conversation.

"Not at all," Thomas replied. "We are finished anyway, what can I assist you with?"

"As you no doubt are aware, I have been given the task of keeping records of materials used and needed," Eric explained. "Also the security on this site. The prior has supplied weapons for us to defend ourselves and that of the church; they are in one of the carts. The problem is Thomas, where do I store them? And, above all,

I need to question the men on their capability in using such weapons."

"The answer to your first question is to erect a wooden structure," Thomas said, after a moment's thought. "Beginning when the carpenters return. The second is that you will have to question each man in turn, but please carry it out when we have our midday meal, we are a little behind in this build as it is."

Nodding his agreement, Eric left Thomas and began his task of book keeping.

He started by counting the layers of stone already laid, what had been issued when work had begun and how many stones laid in a day. Judging by the wetness of the mortar from yesterday and counting the stones at hand, he made the calculations and entered them in the ledger. To calculate the sand and lime used, he asked Amy.

It was clear they needed more stone. The carpenters arrived back by midday, cart laden with thick poles and wood for planks. They were immediately informed by Thomas that they needed to build a hut. The weather was kind that day: there was naught but blue skies, with just a little cluster of fluffy clouds. Eric put it as being early June. Thomas called a break for lunch, and asked if they would all sit together, since Eric had something to say to them all.

Feeling a little awkward and nervy, he began to tell them of the tasks allotted to him, and stressed the point about the weapons.

"How many of you can wield a sword, shoot an arrow, or use a pike?"

None raised a hand.

"Alright," he said. "If you were taught, would you defend this church?"

After some discussion, they all more or less said it would be their wages they would fight for. No church, meant no money. Eric stated that he would speak to prior Gilbert to arrange a day of training. One of the carpenters, named Joshua, said that building a secure home for the weapons would take too long at this present time, and came up with a short term solution.

It was agreed by all, that a shallow, grave-like hole be dug inside the church. A wooden box would be made to line the sides, the lid covered by building materials.

"And it can be done in one hour of the clock!" exclaimed a proud and beaming Joshua.

True to his word, he completed the task in just under the hour, and resumed building the scaffolding with his co-worker. Eric saddled up Beth in mid-afternoon, and set out for the Monastery, hoping to see Prior Gilbert with the idea of training the men. The novice answered Eric's knock on the door.

"I would like to see the Prior if that is possible."

"What is the nature of your request?" the novice asked.

What bloody business has it got to do with you? Eric thought.

"It is to do with weapon training," he said, evenly.

"The Prior is very busy at the moment, reading some paper work he has just received, but I will see if he will grant an audience with you," said the novice, and closed the door.

Bloody upstart, using big words, he mused. Friar Tuck didn't speak like that in Robin Hood!.

The door opened again.

"The Prior will see you, but only keep him for a few minutes," said the novice. "As I said, he is very busy."

Eric followed the upstart to the prior's study. He didn't like this novice one bit, he had a smug face – one you would like to put your fist through.

"Come in Eric, have a seat," the prior indicated a chair opposite his desk. "What can I help you with?"

"Firstly, sir, I have carried out a stock check of materials, and we need more stone. We have enough for three days only," said Eric. "And secondly, sir, I need to teach the men how to use the weapons you kindly supplied."

"Is that all?" Prior Gilbert smiled "I think I can answer both questions in one Eric. It takes five days for the stone to be delivered, if I give the order with the wine merchant, who is arriving by river barge to pick up wine later in the day. That leaves the men three days work. The fourth can be spent learning to use weaponry. The merchant passes by the quarry to the city. Simple.

"I'm afraid I cannot spend more time with you Eric," said Prior Gilbert, rising. "I have to read these papers, copies from the Bishop of Derby. Apparently, King John is being forced by the Barons to sign a charter in a few days time, set up by Stephen, the Archbishop of Canterbury. Something called the Magna Carta."

Eric took his leave, and rode back out to the site. He explained to Thomas the conversation he had with the Prior.

"In that case," Thomas answered, "we will have to get a move on and lay these remaining stones pretty quick. There's much to do apart from just building, Eric, there is scaffolding to be erected. You could give the lads a hand, if you like. More hands, and all that."

Eric was only to pleased to see how middle ages scaffolding was made. In fact, he was excited to be here amongst the clever people of this poor village. If only he could have a modern input. Unlike the shower he devised for Molly and her dad, he knew he had to go along with their way of life, but maybe he could drop a few hints now and again.

Since the morning, the walls had grown two stones higher. They now reached to the top of his head. Joshua it seemed, had recently returned from another trip to the woods for more poles, and was placing them on the ground for sorting. Each pole was roughly seven feet in height; Edward, the other carpenter, was marking each pole roughly one foot from the top and two feet down made another mark. It looked as if there were about a hundred poles in total. The labourers made notches on the marks made. Anthony put holes in the notches – it was like an assembly line, and each worker had a job to do.

Eric was given the task of sawing pieces of pole three feet in length, and in no time at all, he had a good pile. Amy came over to where he was working.

"Earning your keep at last," she said, squatting down beside the cut timber. "I've not to make any more mortar today it seems. This scaffolding is to be finished and erected first, but not today I fear – Thomas will stop work any minute."

Sure enough, in no time at all wagons were hitched and tired and hungry workers piled

172

aboard. Eric, realizing that he hadn't eaten his packed lunch as he pulled the girth tight under Beth's belly, removed the bag, ate a mouthful of cheese, the bread being on the hard side, and tossed the contents over a hedge.

What would I give, to have a hot bath or shower, a pizza, and watch a bit of TV, Eric pondered as he slowly took the road back to the monastery. No. This is the choice I made, and I will stay here. Although it's a nice thought that I can go back if I wish to.

He caught up with the wagons. Although there wasn't work for Amy on the day of the training, she insisted on joining the men on the ride to the site. Eric hoped it was a liking for him, and not to see him make a fool of himself with the men. Amy sat nearby as he gathered the men together in a line, the weapons recovered from the hiding place. He explained how to string the bow with a demonstration, and was pleased that Walter's training didn't let him down.

After each man had mastered the task, let loose a few arrows and retrieved them, Eric was satisfied with the results. The broadsword was a different matter, although he had seen the knights wielding them, he hadn't actually used one, so he went through the motions of parry-thrust and slice in his demonstration: using two hands, and enforcing the need to stand back at least a sword's length. He taught them to use the pommel and cross guard, if possible, on their opponent's head. The pike didn't need a demonstration; it was a simple matter of using the common sense of the man behind it. With the lack of weapons for each man, training took longer than anticipated.

Eric put the men in three sections: archers, swordsmen and pike men, so there would be no confusion when collecting the weapons. Amy was captivated by all this, she just sat and watched Eric go through the training, feeling admiration and ore liking for him as each day passed. As the men dispersed to carry on with their other tasks, she sidled over to him.

"And what role do I play in your training?" she said, smiling.

Eric was flustered at her direct approach, and came out with, "You could maybe carry my quiver?" It was such a daft thing to say, he thought. "I hope you don't get involved," he finally said.

"I could hold something else, instead of your quiver," she giggled, Eric went crimson.

"I would like that," he spluttered, taking her meaning in a vulgar way, but not sure what she meant.

Lunch was called and Thomas joined Eric and Amy.

"Now that all the stone we had has been laid, we need to get the first stage of the scaffolding up before the day is out," Thomas spoke in between mouthfuls of bread and cheese. "If you both could help, seeing as the training has finished, and there's no mortar to be made." He smiled and winked at the them at the same time.

"Gladly, won't we Amy?"

"Of course we will, Thomas," said Amy. "Just show us what to do."

The notched poles fitted together, and Thomas gave them the task to tie strong hemp twine around the joints. The scaffolding went around the inside of the four walls; ladders were erected at each section and finally, the planks were laid on top. Thomas secured each section to the walls by a metal hook, driven into the mortar. Eric was impressed by the end result: it looked fragile, but was sturdy.

Eric tied Beth to the cart on the return to the village, and sat with Amy. During the bumpy ride, he expressed to her how much he disliked living in the monastery, he was pleased to have accommodation, but the chanting was driving him up the wall.

"Why don't you come and live with me?" she exclaimed. "I have a large cottage, stables for Beth, and you could help pay the damned tithe with me."

"Don't get me wrong Amy, I'd love to," he said. "But what would the people of the village say? And the monastery, the Lord of the Manor and so on?"

"I don't much care what people say Eric, but I'm sure if you explained the circumstances to Prior Gilbert, he would understand."

He found eating his supper difficult – Amy's suggestion wouldn't leave his mind. He decided to try and see the prior after his meal. He rehearsed in his mind what he wanted to say, as he made his way to the prior's door. The same snotty nosed novice answered the door. He looked Eric up and down, as if he was a piece of shit that he had just stepped on.

"Yes?" he said, with that irritating tone.

"I would like to see the prior on business."

"What business?"

"My own business, for the prior and me alone," replied Eric, not giving the arsehole any further information.

"Wait," he said, and closed the door.

Some of the job centre people he had had to see when he was signing on, were very much the same as this upstart. Standing outside a closed door was like being summoned to the headmaster's office. The door eventually reopened.

"He will see you, follow me."

"No need," Eric replied. "I know the way," he said, and pushed by him.

"Eric, what news? How did the training go? No bad news at the site I hope?" the Prior said, all in one sentence.

"No, sir, everything is fine. The training went well. It is a private matter I wish to discuss with you, if I may."

Prior Gilbert listened, a smile on his face, as Eric explained the reason for seeing him.

"We can move you to a room further away from the chapel; you wouldn't hear us so much, I'm afraid we can't move the chapel," he laughed. "Seriously, though," he said, with more of a smile more than before, "if you insist on moving in with Amy, you both will suffer the consequences of humiliation from our village, small as it is, and more importantly, Eric, the church will not approve. It could mean the loss of both jobs on the build, and if Amy cannot pay the tithe on the cottage, she will lose it.

"However, there is a way around this, Eric," he said, amused. "I take it you and Amy are fond of each other?"

"Yes, sir," Eric replied.

"And have you consummated the courtship?"

"Err – no!" Eric spluttered. "We haven't had time – I mean – we haven't known each other very long!"

He could feel himself blush.

"I believe you Eric, I didn't mean to pry into your courtship, or embarrass you, but I needed to know," said Prior Gilbert. "The solution, Eric is, marriage."

Eric didn't get much sleep that night, after the prior's summing up.

Bloody hell, marriage! Eric thought, as he lay in his cell. No chance of a quick leg-over in this century – and why did he have to say consummate? Shag would have been better, although I expect shag or leg-over are not terms they use here. However, 'fuck' is centuries old.

"If I were to marry Amy? there's no going back" how could I leave a married woman to support herself financially in a time where women generally couldn't? "I like Amy, and I think she likes me."

After a breakfast of porridge with honey and a slice of cold meat with a noggin of bread, washed down with warm light ale, he was ready to tackle the day ahead. He picked up his lunch parcel from his place at the table and went outside. Beth was saddled and ready for him. The day looked promising: the dawn was breaking with a clear sky. He decided to remember to tip the stable boy who looked after Beth when he got paid.

"Morning," Anthony and Thomas said in unison, as Eric approached the horse.

"Morning," he said. "I hope you get your stone today, directing this at Thomas."

He peered at a contraption hitched up to one of the carts. They began to move out of the yard, this gigantic wooden wheel following, the workers' cart picking up people en-route. Amy appeared on the roadway, nimbly jumping on as it passed. She waved, the noise of all those wheels pounding the hard earth packed road made conversation impossible. Eric felt like an outrider in one of John Wayne's wagon trails, minus the cattle. The wheel reminded him of a smaller version of the Trojan horse entering the city.

Arriving at the site somewhat later than usual, due to the slow moving of that heavy wheel, everyone gathered eagerly around it. Eric stood alongside Amy.

"What did the prior say?" she asked. "Have you spoken to him, yet? Please tell me, Eric."

She held his hand, giving it a little squeeze.

"I will tell you when we have a minute to ourselves," he said.

Thomas directed the driver to put the wheel alongside one of the walls, unhitched the cart, and bade him to go down to the river and await the arrival of the stone, taking two men with him.

"Did you ever see such a fine piece of ingenuity like this in Derby, Eric? Thomas asked, looking proudly at the contraption.

"No, I can't recall that I did," Eric replied, forgetting he still held Amy's hand, and withdrew it quickly.

"Without this tread wheel, the build could not continue. It was invented years ago," Thomas explained. "Clever people, those Romans."

The men began putting together the wooden jib, others making a large wooden pallet for the stone; everyone had a task, overseen by Thomas.

"Seeing as Amy and I have no job at the present, I think we will go along to the river, I will have to sign for the stone anyway," Eric said to Thomas.

Not waiting for a reply, they left the site heading for the lane that led to the river.

Out of sight of the build, Amy grabbed Eric's hand again.

"So will you tell me now? she pleaded.

"Yes," said Eric. "I discussed moving in with you, and gave the reasons. The prior's final word was that if we wanted to do it, we would have to get married."

Amy stopped dead in her tracks.

"Really?" she said, tremulously. "I expected him to say no, but marriage... what was your reply to him?"

"I was a bit speechless, to say the least," Eric confided.

"Well," said Amy, after a moment, "why not? I haven't met anyone like you, certainly not in this village – and I like being with you. Do you feel the same way, Eric?"

"Yes, of course I do," he said. "But we have only known each other for one week, we haven't had much time together."

"But that will change once we're married," she giggled.

"Seriously though, do you honestly think we could make a go of it?" Eric asked, taking Amy's hands in his and looking into her eyes.

"I will if you will," she said, pausing to kiss him. "And before you know it, we will love each other, more than liking one another."

The tenderness of her kiss sealed it for Eric.

"Alright," he said, lifting her off the ground and kissing her back passionately. He released her quickly, feeling the hardness in those stupid skimpy hose he wore.

"That's confirmed it, truly," she said, placing her hand gently on his manhood.

"I didn't think you'd notice," he said, laughing.

The stone had arrived by the time they reached the river, the men were sweating in the hot sun, loading up the cart. Eric approached the barge man.

"I have the authority to sign for the stone," he told him. "Would you be so kind as to deliver another consignment, which would get us to the roof?"

"Don't know when that'll be," the man said. "Another church is going up nearer Derby, the quarry is finding it difficult to supply enough. But for prior Gilbert, I'll do my best, a good man he be."

"Thank you," Eric replied, and began helping the men load the last of the stone onto the cart.

Eric calculated it to be around 9 a.m. when they began heading back to the site. It was getting hot, the track being hard and dry, making it easy for the cart – a different story when it was wet. Amy wanted to walk back, refusing a lift on the cart, so she had the chance of a kiss and a cuddle with Eric, and to discuss their future marriage. Eric was amazed at the transformation of the wheel as they walked onto the site. Like a small boy with a toy, Eric wanted to take in every detail of this medieval building apparatus.

"I'd better begin making mortar," Amy said, "now we have stone. I'll see you later my husband to be," she giggled, and gave Eric's hand a final squeeze.

The stone was being offloaded at different points around the walls as Eric sauntered over to take a closer look at this huge wheel. The wheel itself was positioned in the middle of a flat decked cart; stone was placed on the deck at the rear.

For counterbalance, Eric mused.

The height of the wheel from the floor of the cart to the top was fifteen feet; the cart was another four feet from ground to the floor. It was supported by four, enormous wooden wheels. The crane or jib was built onto the front of the cart: thick long planks were joined together by wooden dowels, a wooden revolving spindle was placed in the middle of the jib and a further spindle was at the end. The rope was tied to the bottom of the wheel, played out under the first spindle, and over the one at the end. The jib was then hoisted up by means of two ropes, which were then secured to two poles fixed at the rear of the cart. The jib was then supported by two fixed poles at the front of the cart; the pinnacle of the jib was at least thirty feet from the ground.

"What do you think of it then, Eric? We'll be ready to start the build again, when your lass has made the first mix," Thomas gave him a wink.

"It's very impressive," Eric said, trying not to look at Thomas.

How many more besides Thomas know of our intentions? thought Eric.

"Would you care to give the tread wheel a go, Eric? When we are ready that is," Thomas offered.

"Right," he replied eagerly.

"Finished the first tub, Thomas," Amy shouted.

"Alright lass," he shouted back and called the builders to their stations.

Men climbed the scaffolding inside, two more were loading the pallet with stone and mortar. All the rest came from their individual tasks to see Eric tread the wheel. He took off his belt and dagger, scrambled onto the cart, then squeezed into the wheel, he suddenly felt like a hamster. Thomas gave the signal, Eric began to walk forward, and to his surprise, the pallet started to lift, effortlessly.

"Stop," the men on the scaffolding shouted, and pulled the pallet onto the wall.

They began unloading, so Eric turned around and began walking slowly on the shout from above, the pallet gently reaching the ground. Pleased with the applause below, he climbed down, retrieved his belt and dagger and stood up, only to be faced with prior Gilbert.

"Works a treat, does it not, Eric? We will have this church up in no time," he declared. "Oh, by the way, have you and Amy had time to consider my proposal?"

"Yes, sir, and we would like to get married soon."

"Good, good," said the prior, happily. "It makes sense. I will notify all concerned, and see if I can fit it in this Sabbath – two days' time. You can wait that long, can't you Eric?" he chuckled, and walked off to seek out Amy.

By lunchtime, everyone on the site was wishing them well; they picked a quiet spot to eat their packed lunch.

"What did the prior have to say?" he asked, nestling in beside Amy.

"Not a lot really, just the usual," she told him. "Do I like you enough to marry you, that sort of thing. He also said, since my parents died, he felt obliged to look out for my welfare, and now

187

it seems he has handed it over to you, He gave us his blessing Eric."

Back in 2020, it would mean spending money one really hadn't got on rig outs, surely that's not the case now, Eric pondered?

Amy broke into his thoughts.

"You will need a change of colour, Eric, maybe a green pair of hose and a red doublet."

"I'll look like a proper pixie," Eric said, without thinking.

"What's a pixie?" Amy said.

"Just a word that came into my head," he flustered.

"I will wear my mother's wedding dress," she said. "Very virginal, and posies in my hair. We need to ask Joshua if he will make us a bed – I only sleep on a straw filled palliasse."

"I agree on the bed," Eric winked, taking a quick kiss, "but I'm not sure on the green hose."

The sun was high at midday, and hot. It seemed to Eric that summer in the 12th century was hotter than back home.

Strange that, he thought, suddenly. I thought about back home, yet this is back, and my home is forward. Anyway, it's bloody hotter.

He was happier now, than he had ever been before. Primitive it might be, but he had friends, and the prospect of being wed – who would have thought it: Eric Middleton, dressed like a pixie, and doing something worthwhile in his once miserable life.

Eric marvelled at the speed the build took on now the tread wheel was in use. He felt a little redundant today, as he sauntered off to find Joshua. Both Joshua and Edward were making curved wooden moulds as he approached.

"Congratulations are in order then, Eric," Joshua grinned. "Quick work, but then I would have snapped her up, had I not been married myself. In't that so, Edward?"

Edward just nodded at Joshua's banter.

"Thanks chaps," Eric replied. "I wondered if you would do me a favour, Joshua."

"Depends on what you have in mind," he said, winking at Edward.

"Would you make us a double bed?" Eric showed Joshua a drawing he had sketched on a blank parchment. "Instead of planks at its base, I would like slats like this," he explained, pointing to the drawing.

"What's be slats then?" Joshua quizzed.

"It's an idea I came up with, same as the word slats," he lied. "They will be more springy, more comfortable than hard solid planks."

"A bed's a bed," said Joshua, scratching his nose. "After all, you's only sleeps in it, and expresses your desires now and then. In't that so?" he said, chuckling and giving Edward a friendly dig in his ribs. "Right you be, Eric, I'll see what we can do. We have to finish these architrave mouldings for the door and windows, then there's mouldings for the pillars to do first. However, your bed shouldn't take long to knock up. Edward can make a start on it now. Be a bit rough though, no time to smooth the edges, if's you be wanting it by the Sabbath."

A delighted Eric shook both their hands. It was only proper that he sought Thomas next, he thought, so he could explain the job he has given to the carpenters. After all, he was the overseer of the work force.

"Would you care to come to the cottage after supper Eric, see what I have – sorry," Amy corrected herself as they neared the monastery, " – what *we* have?" Amy said.

"Of course I will," Eric shouted out, above the din of the cart wheels, getting Beth as close to the wagon as he dared.

Amy jumped off, and disappeared between rows of old thatched dwellings.

"One more meal with you men, then I will be taking my future meals with my wife," Eric announced, proudly, spooning into his mouth the remaining mutton stew in his bowl. It was a little later on and he was eating with Thomas and Anthony in the communal dining hall at the monastery.

"I hear say, she is a good cook," replied Thomas. "You have a good woman there, Eric, take good care of her. We all loves her, is that not right, Anthony?"

"Aye, we do at that."

There was still a little summer light left as he made his way to Amy's cottage, following Thomas's instructions. The cottage was somewhat isolated, built on the corner of a paddock a few minutes from the main street. It was lime washed over daub and wattle; next to it stood an outhouse.

Presumably the stable, Eric thought.

Both roofs were thatched, the little windows were shuttered and were now wide open. Eric heard a bar being lifted from the door inside as he approached.

"Eric!" Amy beamed, flinging the door open. "You made it then," she said, kissing him gently on the lips and pulling him over the threshold. "Well, what do you think of my – sorry – our place?" she corrected herself, as her arms windmilled around the interior.

"Very spacious and clean," Eric complimented her, indicating the newly placed rushes on the floor. "And your fireplace is on the wall, not like so many others, in the centre of the room."

"My father said it would give warmth to the stable next door in winter."

"A wise man, your father," Eric replied, taking in the entirety of the room.

Amy had simple things a family of three would require: table with three chairs, a dresser, pots and pans on a table near the fire place, Amy's palliasse, neatly squared in one corner, clothes piled on a wooden chest.

"Cosy is what it is, Amy," he said. "I can't wait to move in with you."

"Oh, Eric! I'm so pleased you like it – this is like a dream, I just find it difficult to take in," she babbled. "I honestly thought I would never find another man, not in this village anyway. Do you love me, Eric?"

"This much and more," he said, putting his arms around her and kissing her fervently.

"We could consummate the marriage now if you like, Eric," she suggested.

"Not with that door open we couldn't."

Saturday was pay day at the build. Prior Gilbert visited the site around midday and everyone took their turn to approach him, the prior sitting at a makeshift table, the bursar Esop sitting next to him. Esop called out the name and invited the person to sign or make their mark in the book. Eric received seven pence, one silver sixpence, and one penny, Amy was paid the same.

Eric examined his sixpenny piece: it was identical to the one he had come through with, albeit shinier. The use of coins in the village was virtually non-existent, especially among the folk. Barter was the main trade: eggs for this, meat for that; the prior dealt with traders in coins, from the monastery's produce. The stone and lime were also paid for with coinage.

"Don't be spending it all at the market fair," the prior addressed Eric and Amy. "It won't be long before we hold our own fairs, once the church be finished. I will see you both at the monastery tomorrow, for your wedding," were his parting words, as he and brother Esop mounted up and kicked their horses forward.

"What fair?" Eric asked Amy, as they made their way over to where they would eat their lunch.

"The Derby summer fair, just outside the city gates," she told him. "Surely you went to it at some time, Eric."

"No, I can't say that I did," he told her. "My master was a slave driver, didn't have much time for anything."

"Well, if we go, you could show me were you worked," Amy replied, inquiringly.

Taken aback by this sudden suggestion, Eric didn't have a ready answer, but he had to answer nevertheless. Off the top of his head he replied, "It burned down. I was a clerk, as you know, in this ware house, working for a merchant. It happened during the night, so I had no job to go to in the morning. I left, looking for work, and ended up here."

"I'm glad it burned down, Eric, otherwise we would never have met," Amy smiled at him.

"I'm glad I wasn't in it!" Eric laughingly replied.

'So, shall we go, Eric?" Amy asked. "We could buy something for the cottage, or ourselves."

"I don't think Beth could carry two, not at her age," he said, looking thoughtfully at the old, faithful horse.

"No, silly, a cart is leaving the monastery at about four of the clock, giving us plenty of time to wash and change," she told him. "Thomas said it be fitting to finish early the day. So, what do you say, Eric?"

"I say we should go."

The cart was full of villagers: wives, husbands and children. A few of the monastery's armed men accompanied the cart on horseback, at the wishes of prior Gilbert, who was worried that the journey could be interrupted by robbers, knowing people would be going to the fair with money to spend. The journey was bumpy, and hard on the arse. They felt every stone and pothole. As on the cart with Sam, many months before, Eric knew they were getting near to the city due to the stench of it, made worse by the heat of the summer.

On nearing the fair, the cart driver pulled into a paddock and parked under a huge oak tree. Standing on the foot sill of the cart, he addressed his passengers.

"I will be leaving for the monastery at seven of the clock," he told them, sternly. "It be long walks back if you don't be here."

Children jumped down eagerly, running towards the many tents and stalls, ignoring their mothers' pleas for them to come back. Eric lifted Amy down; hand in hand, they headed towards the noise the fair generated. It was a typical medieval fair, full of men walking on stilts, jugglers wearing jester hats, bear dancing, livestock pens, open-fronted tents showing demonstrations by potters, archery contests, and the gambling tricksters, with their three cups and a clay ball.

Amy pointed to a large gathering of people.

"Come on, Eric, let's go and see the attraction," she exclaimed, pulling him towards an open-fronted tent, the flaps parted to reveal a colourful backdrop of painted animals, wizards, people in various poses.

"It's a storyteller, Eric," she told him, excitedly. "You point to one of the symbols, and he tells you a related story – for a small coin of course."

"Let's just hear what others have paid for, and save our money for other things," Eric suggested.

From one stall, Amy purchased cloth for the windows, and a table cloth suggested by Eric. He noticed a trinkets and jewellery stall they had passed earlier, and excused himself from Amy, who was now purchasing thread and

197

needles from yet another stall. Scanning the items on display, he noticed a small, ornate gold ring and a sheathed dagger.

"How much is the ring?" he enquired of the shifty looking stall holder.

"That be a quarter of silver, sir, would fit a nice lady indeed."

"I don't know," Eric pondered. "What about this knife, here," he asked, pointing to the dagger.

"That be half a penny, cheap at that, sir."

Eric made to walk away, but the trader called him back.

"How about, sir, I throw in the dagger for the quarter of silver I asked for?"

"Done," Eric replied and handed over his silver sixpence.

In no time at all, the man handed over his coin minus a quarter of it.

I expect I probably paid too much for the ring, Eric thought to himself. Never did have the flair for bartering.

Both items secured on his person, he sought out Amy.

With minutes before they caught the cart back, Eric purchased pies cheese and bread for them both, knowing he would miss dinner. They sat on the purchased cloth, giving them a little more comfort on the return journey. Eric noticed a church in the throes of being built, a few miles from the city, not as advanced as theirs. Nevertheless, the need for stone for two churches would cause a delay in deliveries if they used the same supplier. Eric wondered whether this was the other church the barge man had told him about.

The journey home seemed shorter than the way in, which may have been because they were all tired and merry, constantly chattering about the fair, Eric and Amy included. The children slept through it all, all huddled together in the middle of the cart.

Eric escorted Amy to the cottage carrying their purchases, once inside, the candles were lit, and Amy covered the table with the new cloth, and they both finished off the remaining food. Eric didn't have any idea of a medieval wedding: did they do the ring thing at the altar?

I will give it to her now, and play the rest by ear, Eric thought.

199

"It's beautiful, Eric, and a wonderful surprise! It fits perfectly," she declared, kissing him long and hard.

"I'm glad you like it, Amy," he smiled. "Do we swap rings and the like at the altar?"

"What a nice thought," she said. "But, no, our wrists will be bound together with a silk white ribbon, prior Gilbert or the Bishop will then bless us in Latin, mass will be said, then we walk from the church to the dining hall as man and wife. Simple really, Eric, nothing to get nervous about."

"You speak as if you've been married before."

"Don't be silly Eric, I have witnessed marriages in the church before, and said to myself, 'One day, Amy, that will be you standing at the altar.' And now, it will be me tomorrow! Eric, I'm so – so happy!" she beamed. "I have a friend, Eric, her name is Eleanor and her husband works in the fields for Lord Moorcroft, she will be my maid of honour. You will like her when you see her."

He was about to leave for the monastery, when a knock on the door interrupted their parting kiss.

"Who could that be at this hour?" Eric lifted the wooden bolt off the door, only to be faced by a smiling Joshua and Edward.

"Sorry to intrude, but we have the bed with us and it has to be put together," Joshua said. "There'll be no time tomorrow and we only have the cart for today."

"You'd best come in then," Eric responded, acting as man of the house already.

Amy, reddening, showed them where it was to be placed. At no time at all, the last dowel was hammered home.

"There you are, fit for King John that be," said Joshua, admiring their handiwork.

"How much do I owe for your labour and the wood? asked Eric, likewise admiring the bed.

"Just think on it as a wedding gift," said Joshua. "The wood be free from the forest and the time given to make it was down to Thomas. All that's left is for it to be christened, so to speak," Joshua said, winking at Amy.

"Well, thanks to you both," she said, hoping the flush had diminished from her face. "We really are grateful – isn't that right, Eric?" she said, averting her glance from the grinning pair.

"We are, and you both made it to my specifications," he said.

When the men had gone, Amy pointed out the strips of wood.

"What are those?"

"They, my love, are called slats, an idea of mine to make the bed more comfy.

Eric was shaken out of his sleep the following morning by the novice monk.

"Prior Gilbert wishes to speak with you after breakfast," he said with some authority, and stormed out of the little room.

"How I hate that little shit," Eric mumbled to himself, and sat up. "I wonder what he wants me for on my wedding day? *Wedding day*," he said aloud. "Bloody hell, I'm getting spliced today!"

He had an appetite for eating a good fry up – wishful thinking on his part, as he entered the mess hall. For saying it was only 6 a.m. (he guessed), the hall was quite full, mostly of monks, but he picked out Thomas and Anthony, and squeezed himself between the two men.

"I want to thank you, Thomas, for giving Joshua and Edward time off to build the bed."

"Think nothing of it," he replied. "Seeing as it's your wedding, Eric, but I wouldn't have given it for anyone else, we are behind in the build as it is."

On his way to see the prior, Eric remembered he'd forgotten to ask Anthony if he had any colourful hose he could borrow.

No time now, he thought. It'll have to wait.

The prior greeted him warmly.

"Sit down, Eric," he said, pointing to a chair opposite. "No doubt you are wondering why I summoned you. I have a simple question for you: do you have a change of clothing?"

"No," Eric answered, a little embarrassed at the question. "I have had neither time or money to find any. It has been arranged by yourself, sir, very quickly – the wedding, I mean."

"Quite so Eric, but you gave me very little choice, living in sin with Amy, as no doubt you would have," he chuckled. "I like Amy, and I felt she had been on her own long enough in that dwelling, so it pleases me, Eric, to wed you both. Now, try this for size," he said, and handed Eric a plum coloured robe and a gold braided rope belt.

This being a Sunday, the chanting didn't stop as Eric made his way back to his room. He also noted that the entrance to the church was being draped in flowers.

I expect it's for our wedding, he thought.

Back in his room, he tried the robe on again, he didn't have a mirror in which to see how daft he looked, but the looseness of the cuffs reminded him of one of the dwarves in Snow White, minus the hat. He could just see the elf-like leather boots.

I suppose it's the trend in this day and age, he thought.

Amy, in the meantime, was cleaning the cottage from top to bottom, with the help of her friend Eleanor. Her palliasse was too small for the bed, so with Eleanor's help, they stitched a new sack and filled it with the chicken and goose feathers that Eric insisted she use. They covered the floor with fresh rushes and a sprinkle of lavender. Amy crushed the remains of the lavender to place in a pomander she wore, hung from the waist under her skirt. It was lunch time. They both ate bread with light ale that would sustain them until the wedding feast.

Eric, on the other hand, had no appetite for lunch. One thing he had to do was to go and see the stable boy who looked after the needs of Beth. He found him cleaning the harnesses in a side room off the stables.

"Sir," he greeted Eric, stopping what he was doing. "Your big day, so I hear."

"Yes it is," Eric replied. "Tell me, what's your name?"

"Arnold, sir."

"Well, Arnold, I would like to give you a gift for looking after Beth for me."

"No need to do that, sir," he said. "The prior looks after me. I sleeps here in this room, takes me meals in the big kitchen and I like looking after the horses."

"How old are you Arnold?" Eric probed.

"Twelve, I think," said Arnold. "Prior Gilbert says I am, anyway. The monastery took me in when I was little, me parents died of the plague."

"I would like to give you this," said Eric, and handed over the sheathed knife.

"Cor!" he exclaimed, wonderment and delight spreading over his small face. "Thanks, sir!" he finally blurted out.

"No thanks needed, lad," said Eric. "How about you tending Beth over at our cottage? She will be stabled there from now on. I will give you pocket money for your troubles."

"No need paying, sir, I will gladly do it for you and Amy!"

"And by the way, call me Eric," said Eric, grinning. "I expect to see you in the hall, after my wedding," were his departing words as he walked away from the lad.

He'd spent longer with the lad than he expected and now, even in the height of summer, he stood shivering in the monks' wash room, trying to scrub himself clean as quickly as possible. A knock sounded on his door, just as he was donning the robe.

"Enter," he said, knowing it was the right word to use.

Prior Gilbert entered the room.

"Nearly ready, are we?" he said. "I thought it better for me to accompany you to the church myself."

"Is it that time already?" Eric said, stomach rumbling.

"Afraid so Eric," said the prior. "You're going to your wedding, not an execution. Hurry up, man."

Crowds gathered outside the church door; Eric was instructed by the prior to stand at the door to await Amy, so they could walk into the church together. Amy arrived some minutes later escorted by Eleanor. Eric took in the interior of the small church as they walked up to the altar: It had a flagstone floor, but no pews as he could judge. People standing to the left and right, allowing just enough room for them to pass. The Bishop of Derby stood behind the altar, beckoning Eric and Amy to come closer. Clearly he wanted to get this ceremony over with as soon as possible, moving from one foot to the other.

Eric thought that he looked like a member of the Ku-Klux-Clan with his white, conical hat and white robe, but at least you could see his sour face.

The Bishop began by tying Eric's left and Amy's right wrist together with a white, silk ribbon, implying the bond between two people, Eric decided, and then began blessing them in Latin.

"Do you, Eric, pledge your life and soul to Amy?"

"I do," Eric replied. Amy replied, "I do," for her part, too.

"Then, in the presence of our Lord God, you are now man and wife."

The monks began chanting Glorias as they both made their way back to the front door, to be greeted by a rain of flower petals, thrown by the cheering women. Eleanor and prior Gilbert led them to the mess hall. Practically the entire village seemed to be seated at the tables. Eric, Amy, Eleanor, the prior and the bishop were seated at the head of the tables; the lord of the manor and his two sons sat next to the bishop.

There was an array of food laid out: bread, cheeses, fowl, wild boar, and of course light ale.

Eric noticed that wine was served at the top table only. Eric was dreading the speech he had to deliver after the meal, but maybe a few tumblers of ale would make it easier. Eleanor, seated next to Eric, had to shout to make herself heard.

"I'm delighted for Amy, that she found someone like you to look after her!"

The din was so loud now; all he could do was to nod to Eleanor's remark. Knives flashed as their owners stabbed at the meats spread out on the tables. He leaned forward, hoping to catch the eye of the Bishop or the prior, in hope they would indicate he made a speech, but they were too occupied in eating and drinking wine. Amy thought it was her he was seeking, and gave him a light kiss on the cheek. He decided at that moment to do it without their approval, took a large swig of ale, and with the hilt of his dagger, banged it down several times on the table, until he had the attention of the startled reception.

Clearing his throat several times, Eric began: "I would like to thank my Lord, the Bishop for officiating at our wedding, prior Gilbert for making this day happen, for allowing the use of his church, and the monastery, for the supply of food and drink, and, above all, for giving me a job," he declared. "Without that, I wouldn't have met my lovely wife. To Eleanor, who has been a good friend to Amy, and to all the friends I have met whilst being on the build."

Eric then sat down to cheers and banging on the tables.

"Blessing cake!" they shouted, in unison.

A little scone like cake was placed in front of the couple.

"This is a fertility cake," Amy whispered to Eric. "Just take a little of it."

To Eric it tasted of seeds – a mixture of sunflower and poppy. The feast finished, it was time for the hand shaking ceremony. That seemed to go on and on. Lord Wilfred and his two sons were the last to leave the top table. Clearly showing signs of too much wine, Lord Wilfred's sweaty hands groped for Amy's, his eyes undressing her from top to bottom.

"I expected you, Amy my dear, to pick one of my boys," he slurred. "Who are both available, with a title to boot. Alas," he joked. "What is done, is done. Eric, my boy," he said, turning to him, "now you are in the folds of the village family so to speak, I will call on you to take up arms if and when necessary."

Not if can bloody well help it, Eric thought to himself.

"Of course," my Lord he said. "I will be at the new church if need be."

At last, they were able to leave the hall; outside Eleanor and her husband waited for them. He was introduced as Seth, a very shy but likeable chap, and they were to accompany them home.

Will we ever be on our own, Eric thought.

Nearing their cottage door, Seth spoke for the first time.

"You can count on us if need be," he said.

"That's very kind of you," Eric said, opening the door. "Goodnight."

Seth grinned, sensing his impatience to be alone with his new wife.

"Bye – and thanks for everything!" Amy said, waving them off.

Picking her up, Eric carried her into the house.

"What did you do that for?" Amy laughed, as he lowered her to the floor.

"It felt like the right thing to do," he said, realising that this was something else they didn't do in this century.

With a cheerful fire burning, even though it was a warm early summer evening, the cottage had a warm, intimate glow, projecting dancing patterns around the room. Eric went over to the far wall to inspect the bed, not having got a chance when the lads had delivered it. It was perfect, and the slats gave it a little spring as he bounced on it, Amy was putting cold meats and cheeses retrieved from the reception onto a cold granite slab, and covering them with a damp muslin cloth.

"Shall we have an early night, Mrs Middleton?" Eric said, tapping the bed with his hand, and adding that it was a working day tomorrow.

"Alright," Amy said. "That is, if you are not hungry after that feast."

She blew out the candle on the table.

"I am hungry, but not for food," said Eric, stripping off his clothes and dropping them where he stood. He slipped under the bed covers quickly.

Amy made her way over to the bed, guided by the light of the fire, and more sedately began to undress, folding her wedding dress neatly, and putting it back in the trunk, the rest of her clothes she placed on the lid, sliding under the cover she reached for Eric.

Their mouths melted into one another, her tongue probed, duelled, entwined with his. Her taste was slippery sweet, warm and soft utterly wonderful to Eric. Still kissing her ardently, he moved on top, blood now pounding and rushing to his loins. He wanted so much to savour the moment, take his time, but that didn't happen. Amy was guiding him home, her pelvis rising to meet his thrusts, it was sheer lust, but it was wonderful. They remarked many hours later, among their giggles, how comfortable the bed was.

Eric awoke to the same dancing patterns on the wall, as he remembered from the night before. Amy had washed, changed into her working clothes and made up the fire; its sole purpose was to heat water in a cauldron, which was suspended over the fire. She was now removing the pot and pouring some in a bowl for Eric.

"Good morning, my husband. I thought I would rise early," she said, as she noticed Eric was yawning and stretching. "There is water and a clean cloth to wash," she added, indicating the bowl perched at the end of the table. "Would you like cheese and bread? The latter being a little stale I'm afraid. The warm ale by the fire hasn't gone sour yet."

Eric, just for a second, let his mind drift back to a nice hot bath, a hot breakfast and that long yearned for a cup of tea or coffee.

"Eric?" Amy said again, bringing him out of his reverie.

Eric washed and dressed in his work clothes, taking just a little time to eat some cold meat and bread, washed down with the warm ale.

"We should be given the day off," quipped Amy, damping down the fire and lifting the water pot off the metal bar.

"That should be my job, now that we are married," Eric said.

He was embarrassed that Amy had just about done everything, even parcelling up their lunch.

"Living on your own for so long, it's a force of habit," she laughed. "Don't worry, my love, I will make sure I leave you something."

Eric being the last to leave, secured the cottage, kissed Amy, and made for the stable to saddle up Beth, Amy meanwhile, walked towards the monastery to get her usual lift on the dray cart. Eric was shocked to see the horse saddled and waiting. Arnold was mucking out the stall.

"I have made up a nose bag of oats for Beth, sir, and a little hay," the boy told him. "Both are strapped on the saddle."

"Thank you, Arnold, I didn't expect you to start so early," said Eric. "Clearly, you were up at the crack of dawn, and I appreciate it, but you don't have to come over this early, I can saddle up Beth."

"It's no bother, sir. I gets up early at the monastery as it is, I wants to do it for you," said Arnold, touching the precious dagger on his belt.

"Well, its alright by me," said Eric, mounting up and setting off to catch up with Amy and the cart.

As could be expected, Eric and Amy got a bit of ribbing on the way to the site, all good natured though.

On arrival at the site, it was clear they had been robbed of stone, sometime over the Sabbath. On closer inspection, it appeared a cart had been used, leaving deep wheel ruts in the soft ground next to the stacked stone. Luckily, only half of the pile was missing, so they could still start work.

"Theft be theft," remarked Thomas. "The culprits must be bought to heel."

"I totally agree," said Eric. "Leave it to me. You stay here and carry on with the build."

After all, security is my job, Eric thought to himself.

After explaining to Amy that he was going to have a look around to try to pick up some clues, Eric kissed her and rode off. He followed the cart tracks from the site, which took him onto the road to Derby; he pulled Beth to a stop as more tracks intermingled. It was obvious to Eric that they headed towards Derby, because of the angle at which the cart joined the road.

Why take just stone? he wondered. We had oak beams made up, ready for the roof, bags of lime, clay – everything you would require in a builders yard, Eric said to himself.

Then he remembered the church he had seen just outside of the city. He mounted up, and headed Beth towards Derby; he had his sword and dagger, but no protective clothing at all. Finally, at Beth's slow pace, he could just make out the church at a distance.

Getting closer without being seen, he decided to leave the horse tied up in a gully off the road, and moved in on foot. Crawling on his belly and peering over a small hillock, Eric took stock of the situation in front of him. The church was behind in build, as theirs was. He also noted four big horses grazing in the adjacent field, the cart nearby, and two separate piles of stone. Obviously, one of them could have come from the church at Skelton.

The builders were working, yet two men were sitting on a bale of straw, wearing half armour, armed with swords. Shields and pike staffs lay nearby.

"Shit," Eric said to himself, knowing full well what could be achieved by the swords and those deadly pikes. He had witnessed many men's entrails falling out of their stomachs at Bosworth – his own bowels were murmuring now, just at the thought of it. Sweating with sheer fear, he began running back to Beth, hoping he was not seen by anyone. Putting the horse in a fast trot, which was all that could be expected from old Beth, since a canter might kill her, he set off.

With a few hundred yards between them, he managed a backward glance.

"So far, so good," he said to Beth.

He could see no dust clouds in pursuit, so he brought her to a walking pace.

Some forty minutes later, they ambled onto site, both sweating and in need of liquid refreshment. Eric dismounted, loosened the girth from around Beth's belly, then gave her a bucket of water. Her thirst quenched, he tied the nose bag of oats on her muzzle and set out to find Thomas. On seeing Eric return, Amy took a pitcher of ale over to him, he gulped down his thirst quickly, wiping his mouth with the back of his hand.

"Thanks, my love," he said to Amy. "I needed that."

Thomas was directing the fitting of the windows, and by means of the tread wheel lifting the oak beamed roof frames into place.

"So, what have you found out?" he asked, leaving the tasks in hand to Edward and Joshua.

"I believe it was men from that church build near Derby," he told him. "I observed them at a safe distance. They had two separate piles of stone – I judged one to be ours. There were a few men labouring, but what concerns me more is that they have two men at arms protecting the build and two battle horses nearby. Their church is much further behind ours," said Eric, still a little out of breath from the ride.

"It would not be a problem to identify our stone," said Thomas. "Anthony said as how he marked some stone ready for carving."

"That would make it easier, but do you honestly think they would hand it back without a fight?" said Eric, now fully composed. "We couldn't take on those men at arms. I will think of something over lunch."

Amy joined Eric for lunch. It was a hot day. Covered with lime dust, she dropped onto the grass beside him. They sat on a small grass mound near to Beth, who was trying to get the last remnants of oats from her nosebag. Eric removed the bag, and she went on, happily tugging on the grass.

"What are you going to do, Eric?" Amy said, handing him his lunch.

"I'd better inform the prior," he said. "After all, he paid for the missing stone. Then I will have to come up with something, it's my responsibility after all," he added, taking a swig of warm ale from the jar, and wiping his mouth with the back of his hand. He kissed Amy on the lips, smiling. "I can do this any time, any place, now that we are married."

"Yes you can, my husband," she grinned. "But I have my job to do – I will soon be finished with mixing mortar, then I don't know what Thomas will have me do next."

"Something more fitting a married woman," Eric joked, kissing her once more before she left.

Eric still hadn't come up with a way of getting the stone back, when a little later after lunch, the prior and his entourage – consisting of two monks –entered the site. Taking in the progress of the build, he congratulated Thomas on his work, dismounting. He walked over to Eric and frowned.

"All is well, I hope," he said. "You look somewhat troubled – I can read your face. Tell me what ails, Eric."

Eric began to explain all, leaving nothing out.

"I feared something like this would happen," the prior nodded, thoughtfully. "My guess is that the authorities funding that church know nothing of the theft, and the stone mason and his builders would benefit by claiming for a delivery of stone that didn't happen, pocketing the money. It's an old and common swindle. We need to get the stone back, Eric, but how?"

"We could take on the builders in a fight," Eric said. "But the experienced men at arms are another matter," Eric expressed, proudly.

"Let us try to solve this without bloodshed, Eric," the prior responded. "If, as you say, Anthony marked some of the stone for carving, then that is our hope of proving it is ours. The only problem is, Eric, those men at arms and their mason, who I guess is in league with them."

"What about this, sir," Eric proposed. "You ride to Derby and confront the abbot, get him to accompany you back to the build. In the meantime, me and the men here will arm ourselves, surround their church, and await your arrival, just in case they become stroppy."

"Stroppy?"

"It's – um – just a word I picked up, sir," Eric fabricated. "I think it means difficult. Anyway, then you could play your trump card, by showing the abbot the marked stones."

"Sometimes I think you talk in riddles, Eric," said Prior Gilbert. "'Stroppy', 'trump' – however, I think your plan just might work. I will leave now. Time is of the essence, they might have used the stones already. Give me time to get to Derby Eric, then set out and deploy your men – and God be with you."

After the prior had left, Eric went over to where Thomas was giving instructions for the roof beams to be lowered into place, with the help of the tread wheel. Eric explained the plan on how to get the stones back, and about how they were to stop work and take up arms. Having given the prior enough time to reach the city, they prepared to leave. With the men now all armed and sitting on the cart, Eric mounted Beth. They left Amy to guard the site, much to her disapproval, along with two of the older labourers.

A good half mile from the church, he halted the cart.

"From here, we walk," he told them.

The men jumped down, all jabbering like schoolchildren on a nature tour.

"Listen up," he told them, sternly. "It is paramount we keep silent from here on. We must surround the church and take them by surprise. I will deploy each one of you at a station around the building, so, string your bows, now."

Eric told the driver of the cart to wait as they tried to get as close to the site as is possible.

With the men in position, Eric concealed himself opposite the men at arms, an arrow resting on his bow, the shaft tipped with a bodkin able to pierce chainmail.

"No one is to loose an arrow until I give the order," Eric told each man.

It became hot and sticky, just sitting and waiting. They seemed to have been there for hours. The sweat was running down Eric's face and neck, mainly through fear rather than heat.

Why are they not here? Eric thought, watching the building site carefully.

As if is thoughts were answered, a group of riders entered the site. The prior along with the abbot dismounted, but the rest of the retinue remained mounted. The abbot informed a labourer to fetch the master mason, who it appeared, was working on the other side of the church. The commotion brought the men at arms to their feet. Swords drawn, they approached the abbot, who was close enough for Eric to overhear their conversation.

"What is this all about, sir?" inquired one of the men.

"All will be revealed soon, my good man," answered the abbot.

The master mason ambled across to the waiting party.

"You wish to see me, my lord abbot?"

"Yes I do, Charles," he said. "You recently took a purchase of stone, which you expect me to pay for, is that correct Charles?"

"Yes sir."

"Would you show me this stone?"

"This one, my lord" said Charles, and pointed it out.

The prior joined the abbot in examining the top layer of stone; he turned over the top stone, only to reveal the markings in charcoal made by Anthony.

"Then how do you account for those drawings?" he asked.

"I don't know," stammered the mason.

"I know, and I will tell you," thundered the abbot. "You stole these stones from prior Gilbert's church to make extra money for yourself, and those who accompanied you!"

"Those markings mean nothing, they could have been made by anyone," insisted the mason. "Anyhow, I have these men at arms to back me up, and you only have this small retinue of monks."

"I wouldn't be too sure on that," implied prior Gilbert, and lifted his arm in the air – a signal for Eric to loose an arrow.

Eric saw the arm go up, gulped, drew back on the string, aimed and let fly. The arrow landed between the men at arms feet.

"See," said the prior. "That arrow could have killed you if I had wanted it to. You are surrounded by skilled archers."

The prior now lifted both arms up. Eric stood and bid his men to do the same. The men at arms let their swords fall to the ground, a clear sign of submission.

"Now, what has transpired hear today is a clear case of theft," said the abbot. "However, since prior Gilbert will get his stone back and I haven't yet parted with the Diocese money, we will forgo the usual punishments. You ought to be ashamed of yourselves, stealing while building a church. You, master stone mason, will leave this site immediately – and if you should return to give vengeance on the prior, his men, or their church, then I will alert the sheriff of Derby to hunt you down. You will surely die a thief at his hands, that you are.

"The men can stay on the build," he continued, running his eyes over them. "I'm sure there is a budding mason amongst them to take your place. And you two gentlemen," he said, addressing the men at arms, "will leave this site, not to return. I'm sure there is plenty more money elsewhere to be got as the mercenaries that you are."

When the stone was back on the cart, the men perched on top singing a victory song, they all headed back to their place of work. The prior rode alongside Eric, the retinue taking up the rear.

"Are you pleased your plan succeeded, Eric?" he asked.

"Yes, sir," he replied with pride.

"Incidentally, that was a very good shot of yours, Eric."

"I don't think so, sir," Eric said. "You see, I was aiming for his chest!"

With that, they both burst out laughing.

Months passed without further incidents and the church was nearing its completion. A wall was built around the church, areas allotted for a graveyard, and a bigger area created for fairs and markets. Prior Gilbert had prayed for so long for this church to be built.

"Our own parish church, Eric," he said, whilst explaining the building's importance to him as they sat together looking at the wonder of it.

Markets would be one day per week, and the fairs would last a month.

"Imagine the revenue it will bring to the parish, Eric," he said, enthusiastically. "The stall holders can camp in that adjacent field," he pointed it out. "Lord Wilfred of the manor will have to appoint a priest and a parsonage house to go with the job."

"Why can't you appoint a priest from the monastery?" Eric asked glibly.

"It is common practice to appoint a commoner by birth, not labourers or serfs tied to the land," the prior replied. "Even you could do it Eric. Think on it," he said, and he smiled. "Wages come from parish lands. The tithe, as you are

228

aware, Eric, is one tenth of a person's earnings, taken to support the church. It is divided between the priest, church maintenance fund, the poor, and not forgetting the Bishop. An income would also come from services like weddings, funerals, baptisms and such. It's endless, Eric, endless.

"The nave and tower belong to the people of the parish," he continued to ramble. "Courts will be held in the nave, but the chancel and altar belong to our Lord. The tithe will be paid to the priest in the nave, also a meal will be given to the poor of the parish that have paid their scot – their taxes. So, Eric, there you have it. Here endeth the first lesson."

On that last remark, they both chuckled. The prior left for the monastery, leaving Eric to ponder to himself.

The phrase 'scot free' must come from paying taxes, then, he thought.

Anthony was just putting the finishing touches to one of his tall stone pillars inside the church, using a coarse brush and water. Glancing back, he noticed Eric approach.

"Alright, Eric. What do you think of our handiwork, then?"

"Fantastic," he replied. "Fit for a king. You, Thomas, the carpenters and labourers have done a great job."

"You are forgetting your Amy, Eric," said Anthony, grinning. "Without her mixes we couldn't have done it. How is she, by the way?"

"Grand Anthony, thank you," Eric replied. "Complains of being tired a lot. I suppose pregnant women are all the same. Could I borrow a chisel and mallet for a minute, Anthony? I want to make a mark on something."

"Help yourself from that bag."

"Thanks."

Outside, he made a small signature in the corner of the stone door frame: 'EM'. He smiled to himself as he did it, like 'Smiffy wus here' on the toilet walls back home.

Months passed and Amy was only days from giving birth; Eric had built extra rooms onto the cottage, separated the kitchen from the bedroom, and added a fireplace in the

230

bedroom. He made a habit of moving the cess pit frequently. With the manure from Beth, he fertilized a vegetable garden.

The baby arrived with the assistance of the monastery Infirmary and Amy's best friend; he was named Noah after the story in the bible. Eric was so proud, he would give anything to see his mother's face right now – which got him to thinking.

I could go back quickly and only see them for one day.

He tried to work out how long had he been away: then adding time to that, if his calculations were correct, they would be very old now, maybe even dead. He made his decision; he would go when Amy and Noah were strong enough to be left on their own.

CHAPTER SIX

Eric made his excuses to Amy, saying he was going into Derby. The church was almost finished, and he was in limbo as to his next appointment with the prior. Making his way on foot to the church, which could be seen from miles away because of its high tower, Eric had that deceitful feeling again. It was a feeling he had had many times before, lying to these good people – and especially to Amy. He consoled himself that he would be back before the day was out.

It was hot, and it seemed to take ages to get to the church. He entered the corner of the field, coin in hand and he lay down, looking up at a clear blue sky. Eric closed his eyes and rubbed the coin.

This time the feeling he encountered was not like the other times: he seemed to be falling instead of doing the usual cartwheels. The motion stopped, and he opened his eyes – he was back in the dark drift. Instinctively, he found his belongings. The growth at the entrance was thicker, making it darker inside.

He used the spade to clear the opening, leaving the spade inside. He crawled through and managed to stand up on wobbly legs. It was a cold day, the sky was an unusual colour grey, and the clouds seemed lower to Eric, like a huge blanket.

It felt strange to be wearing shoes again. He sensed a stillness to the area, and the field was not green, but an ashen colour.

Something was very wrong Eric feared, he made his way to the church. The door was open and he peered inside. It obviously hadn't been used for some time, dust covered everything. Backing out, he looked to the corner of the stone framed door, and smiled to himself. There, etched into the stone, was 'EM.'

Well that hasn't changed, he thought. The grooves have darkened with age, but never the less, it's mine.

The farm buildings looked drab and there were no dogs barking, like they did when anyone got near. There were no animals in the fields either. Eric now began to feel panic engulf him. He carried on walking to the beginning of the built up area of houses and looked down the street.

Nothing. He was alone and afraid. The trees were bare of leaves, and everywhere he looked was covered in a fine coating of dust.

"Holy shit," he said frightening himself. "They've only gone and done it!"

Eric didn't need persuading: in his mind this was nuclear fallout dust. Heart thumping in his chest, he ran back to the drift as fast as his legs would take him. He paused at the entrance and headed back towards the church. He had to visit the graveyard and look for a particular headstone first. He found it, again the inscription was black with age, but he managed to trace the indentation. Amy Middleton, Eric Middleton and Noah Middleton. He stared at it. He couldn't make out the end of the inscription, just the first half of the year, '12--'

Bloody hell, Eric thought. I'm dead. I will be all the sooner if I don't move from here quick!

Back inside the drift, he sat down and tried to figure out just what he had seen.

"I hope to God I haven't been contaminated," he said aloud.

He felt okay, but then it could have a delayed effect.

Bloody hell – hang on a minute, his mind was telling him, you've just seen that you died along with Amy and Noah, so you couldn't have been affected with radiation. I wonder what would be worse, dying of radiation or dying of the numerous plagues that were in the twelfth century? Either way, I'm doomed in this century, so it's back to the twelfth with my wife and son. Am I the only one left in this century?

"Here goes," he said and rubbed the coin.

He opened his eyes to a dazzling bright day, a big contrast from where he had just left. His dress was as before, there was money in his pouch, yet something was wrong. The church was there, he could hear laughter coming from the adjacent field to the church, and he could see the tops of tents. Making his way over to the noise, he could see that it was a fair, but prior Gilbert had said it wouldn't begin for a few months after the church was completed.

But I have only been away for a day, he thought, desperately.

Eric was hungry and thirsty. He made his way over to a pie stall, purchased a pie and while he was eating, he sought out someone who could give him some answers to quell his fears. The ale man would know. He was dipping tankards into a barrel so Eric took his tankard and thanked him.

"Would you know if Prior Gilbert is visiting the fair?" Eric casually asked him.

"Prior who?"

"Gilbert," Eric repeated.

"Don't know as I do," he said. "It's prior Stephen down in that there monastery."

Eric thanked him, and moved on. He was now beside himself with worry.

What's bloody happened?

Sweating with anxiety, he headed for the church. He found it cooler inside; a priest was at the altar, a scattering of people on knees praying. Approaching the priest, Eric had to give the old tale of amnesia again.

"I have heard of a prior Gilbert, lad, but that was many, many years ago, and we are in the year of King Henry III, 1265," he said. "I hope your memory comes back to you soon, lad. I will pray for you."

Eric said thanks, and hurried out of the church. He ran round to the graveyard found what he was looking for.

"Christ, I'm still bloody dead!"

I need to go back and try again, he thought. I'm roughly fifty eight years further on. Somehow there seems to have been a slip in time – maybe due to the nuclear explosion. Either way, I have to get back to Amy and Noah, they are all I've got in this world.

Back in the tunnel, he felt very, very lonely. For some strange reason he was sweating, yet the drift was cold.

All this to-ing and fro-ing must effect me, somehow, he thought. I've grown a beard, and my hair is longer, but other than that I don't feel older. How do I get back to the proper time?

He began to panic.

If there was a slip in time and I went too far forward by standing in the same position as always, would it make any difference if I moved down the wall a little? he pondered. Sounds a bit far-fetched, but I have to try.

Inching his way down the wall and hoping this would knock the right amount of years off, he began rubbing the coin.

Well the church *was* there he noted, as he opened his eyes, however, the stink around him was overpowering. He was lying next to a cess pit. Jumping up quickly, Eric looked to see if he had any shit on his clothes.

"What arsehole put a shit heap here?" he shouted out, to no one in particular, only himself. "This is not right. Christ, what do I do now?"

Eric was beside himself with panic, he began pacing forward and back. He needed to know what year this was.

He didn't see anyone about to ask. There were no tents and no market. He sought out the church again, but there was no one inside. The day was heavy with dark clouds threatening rain, and cold – even colder in the building. He ran outside, then to the graveyard.

"No headstone," he said, feeling oddly relieved. "Which indicates I'm further back."

Eric sat down with his back to another headstone.

"I'm going around in bloody circles," he complained, to the open air. "If I go down to the village, or monastery, and start enquiring, they would want explanations as to my long absence. If it's some years, say, fifteen or twenty years, it would be tragic for Amy and Noah. I wouldn't have a logic explanation. Bloody hell, what a mess! Why did I want to go back in the first place?"

He had no alternative but to go back and try yet again, lying as close to the shit heap as he dared without getting shit on him, he closed his eyes and rubbed, and prayed. Once again back in the dark and isolated drift, Eric rummaged in his bag, and pulled out the relics that had taken him on those earlier travels in time. He started to day dream, and then threw them back in his bag.

I just have to get back to my family, or die trying, he mused. A thought occurred to him: what if I went into the church and prayed? Why did that come into my mind? Eric thought. It would be a bit hypocritical, I've never been in a church before, only at one of my mates' brother's weddings. Still, there's no harm in trying. If that doesn't work, then I shall take the musket ball, and die in France or Portugal, he thought to himself.

The church door was open, inside everything was covered in a film of dust. He walked along to the altar, treading on the flagstones he had witnessed being laid. Eric knelt in the dust, and prayed.

"Let's hope that helps," he said aloud, knowing he was the only one to hear it. The font was just to his right as he was leaving; a little water was still evident at the bottom. "Holy water," he said to himself and submerged the coin.

Positioning himself on the wall, he closed his eyes, and this time prayed to see Amy and Noah again, he rubbed the coin. He was aware of lying down, eyes closed. There was no smell and the sun warm on his face. He wanted to open his eyes, but at the same time he was frightened of being disappointed again. He could hear voices, faint, but clearly people's voices.

"Well, it's now or never," he said, and opened his eyes.

The voices were coming from the direction of the church, now standing upright, he checked himself: he was in the same code of dress, and peering inside his money pouch he found it contained roughly the same amount as he left with.

Eric felt weak in his movements, as he began to walk towards the church. As he got nearer he could make out men on the top of it, putting the final touches to it, he surmised. His heart began thumping in his chest the closer he went. He saw Thomas, gesticulating with his arms, shouting instructions to the men on top. He bounded forward, throwing his arms around Thomas, taking him unawares.

"Take it easy lad!" he gasped. "Have you been and got your Amy pregnant again? Is that what this is about – or have you taken a likin' to me all of a sudden?"

"Nothing like that," Eric beamed. "It's a long story Thomas, but to cut it short, I fell asleep. It being such a nice day, I decided to walk here, got tired, sat down and dozed off. I had a horrible dream, Thomas, that my Amy and Noah, the prior, you and the men here all died of a mysterious illness, leaving me alone. Then I woke up, not knowing whether it was a dream or reality. When I saw you I couldn't help myself, knowing it was only a dream, sorry."

"Well, I'm glad it were only that, Eric lad," said Thomas. "Stay and get a ride back with us on the cart."

Jumping down off the cart, Eric said his goodbyes to the men and raced home. Throwing the door wide open he made for Amy, who was playing with Noah on the flagstone floor. Eric couldn't stand rushes, and so had laid the stones soon after they were married. He knelt down and smothered Amy with kisses, stifling her words. Then he made for Noah, doing the same to his son, only to make him cry.

"Eric, what's come over you?" Amy asked, looking puzzled.

After he had stopped embracing and kissing his dear family, he began to tell her the story he had told Thomas.

"Well, I think you have had too much sun my love, but I wouldn't mind if you were to walk to Derby again," she said and, with that, they both burst out laughing, kissing again.

The church was almost finished, except for the laying of the flagstones. Prior Gilbert was like a child with a new toy, demanding that each and everyone involved with the build should lay the floor. A day was decided, which found them all gathered in the church, each person deciding where his or her stone should be placed. They removed the weapons and placed them on the cart, and then each stood on the earth floor, indicating the spot they would like their flag to be laid.

Four labourers plus Thomas and Anthony brought in the slabs. When it came to Eric and Amy's turn, he requested Amy's to be placed near the font and his at the altar. Prior Gilbert was puzzled at Eric's choice, but decided to say nothing at the time.

"I would like Eric and Thomas – and of course Amy and little Noah – to stay behind when all have left," requested the prior.

The inside of the church was quiet and seemed hollow, now all the workers had left. Eric felt a funny feeling inside, more so when he neared the altar or the font. With Noah perched on his shoulders, Eric followed the small party outside.

"I want your opinions as to where we should locate the graveyard, and the site of the impending markets and fairs," said the prior.

Eric voiced his choice of the site for the graveyard, from his experience, which the prior accepted; Thomas indicated the area of pasture land for the markets; Amy suggested the fair to be the other side of the road, as it could otherwise be too noisy for the parishioners inside. The prior had his input, but agreed on all counts except one, which was where to put the cess pit. The prior was adamant that it should be as far away from the church as possible, and pointed to the far corner of the large adjacent pasture.

So, it was prior Gilbert who was the arsehole that put it there, Eric said to himself, and laughed inwardly.

Over the coming months, the wall surrounding the graveyard was completed and the nave was set aside for the court sessions as the prior had indicated. There were no trestles or pews, people knelt on the flagstones to pray, or stood. There was no bell, or clock in the tower, they would come later no doubt. The bishop of Derby came to bless and sanctify the church and graveyard. Tables were laid in the market area and food, ale, and wine from the monastery were plentiful. The entire village turned out, all that remained was to find a priest.

That evening, having been well fed and watered, Noah was put to bed, totally exhausted from running around with other children at the church. Noah was given the good looks of his mother, and my dark hair. A robust child, finding amusement those children found in this period.

"What job is left for me, now that the church is completed?" Eric posed the question to Amy.

"Maybe the prior will have something for you. You have been loyal to him, my dearest."

"What I would like Amy, is to do something for myself."

He made an excuse that he was going to check Beth, and walked outside to the stable. What he wanted was to have a minute to himself. Beth was pulling down on a hay net, she turned when Eric approached.

"Hello old girl," he said and gently stroked her muzzle.

He went inside, and with a wooden pitch fork, began to lay fresh straw for her bedding, gave her a few oats then closed the door. It was getting dark as he made his way to the privy for a piss, thinking all the time of what he could do. He knew of one job on offer, that was, to be a priest of the church.

In a sense, he thought, it was the church that brought me back, and then there was the strange feeling he got when he was inside.

Dismissing the thought from his mind, he decided to move the midden to another spot and fill in the hole, before it got too full. Amy had warmed up some ale and laid out bread and cheese for their supper when Eric came through the door.

"Do you think I would make a good priest?" Eric blurted out over their evening meal.

"Are you thinking of applying for the post, then?" Amy responded.'

"Well, no, I just wanted your opinion, that's all."

"I think you would be a fine priest, with the proper training, of course." She laughed, and added, "Would that make me a priestess, then?"

At the crack of dawn, Eric slipped out of bed, trying not to wake Amy or Noah. In the kitchen he drank a mouthful of stale beer.

I've got to get used to this beverage, like it or not, but what I would give for a mug of tea right now, he thought.

Outside was chilly – it was the latter part of summer. He noticed pink clouds forming on the horizon, which could be the making of a nice day. As he approached the corner of the cottage, the unmistakable aroma of steam mixed with manure greeted him. Arnold was mucking Beth's stall out.

"Morning, sir," he called, as he noticed Eric.

"You don't have to come in so early Arnold, it can wait a while longer."

"I likes to get the mucking out of all the horses early sir, that way I can have a good breakfast, and take it easy a bit afore I cleans the tack ,sir, and do a spot of grooming," said Arnold, cheerfully.

"You do a good job, Arnold, and I appreciate it. So do the monastery, no doubt. Here," Eric pushed a few pennies in his hand. "Get Beth saddled up for me whilst I nip back and get a bite to eat."

He rekindled the fire, and set a pan of milk by the side. Noah liked barley with warm milk and honey, while Amy would share some cold meat and bread with Eric. He woke Amy gently, by kissing her tenderly on the lips. She smiled, stretched and pulled him onto the bed.

"Not now, sweetheart, I have Beth saddled," he told her, "I will have a bite to eat with you and Noah, then I'm going to ride to the church."

Noah came into the room and jumped on the top of them.

"Alright, that's it," Eric said jokingly.

The top of the sun was now visible on the horizon as Eric took a slow ride out to the church. He let Beth graze the pasture, along with four other horses, one he recognised as belonging to prior Gilbert. The men turned in unison, as Eric entered the church.

"Good morning to you Eric, what brings you here? the prior asked.

"I came to marvel at the work that's been done."

"Splendid Eric, I was just giving Lord Wilfred and his sons a tour," said Prior Gilbert. "We were just discussing finding a priest."

"It seems you are without work now, Eric, anything in the offing?" Lord Wilfred asked.

"No, my Lord."

"Prior Gilbert here tells me it is a job that would suit you. He speaks very highly of you, Eric."

"Thank you, my lord," Eric said, feeling a little uncomfortable.

"This church," the prior went on, "will see the events of so many happenings over the Centuries to come, Eric."

"It surely will, sir. It surely will," Eric smiled, remembering only too well the future that this church would see. The party left, leaving Eric to witness that feeling again, as he approached the altar. It was a strange, warm feeling.

Why? Eric wondered. Was it because the church had brought Eric back to his family, or was it trying to tell him that he belonged here in this church? He felt the same, warm feeling as he passed the font on his way out. The church now after several months of completion, was just an empty structure. Sad really, since all that vigour went into building it. Eric in the mean 'while, helped the bursar with the monastery accounts, to make ends meet. The money he and Amy saved was dwindling fast. It was evident the church was losing money.

It was at a service in the monastery, that the prior was delighted to inform the village that the first market was coming to Moorcroft. Apparently word had spread in Derby that the church was up and running, minus a priest. The prior set the date, sending as many monks to Derby as he could spare to put notices up around the city.

"Maybe we could sell some of the vegetables from our garden, Eric," Amy said as they were about to leave.

"That would help, seeing as we have no proper income," Eric replied.

"Hold on a minute, will you," prior Gilbert said catching up with them. "Have you considered the post, Eric?"

"What post is that, then?" Amy said to Eric.

"It's just employment the prior here offered me," he said, looking at the prior with an expression that said he hadn't spoken to Amy about it.

"Don't let me keep you good people, then," he said and ruffled Noah's hair, who didn't like that one bit. He ran on in front of Amy and Eric.

Amy tackled Eric, as soon as they were indoors about the job offer.

"He said I would make a good priest, and that a parsonage went with it," he admitted. "The salary is sufficient."

"Well?" Amy was quick to respond.

"I neither said yes or no," he said. "I haven't been a church person Amy, and it seems a bit hypocritical to begin now."

"Why don't you speak with him, Eric, you get on so well together," she suggested. "Imagine living in a parsonage – we would be that little bit higher than the average village person."

"Now you're being a snob," Eric said, ending the conversation on light banter.

The privy was now smelling strongly; the warmer the day, the more pungent it became. Noah followed Eric out the door.

"This is no place for a young lad," Eric chided him. "Go on, get back to your mother."

The young boy's lip drooped and he scuffed the ground, hands in pockets. He didn't protest as Eric had imagined he might.

"Alright, tell you what, let me do the privy and I will let you ride on Beth, how's that?"

Noah didn't need telling twice, he was back inside in a flash.

Eric dragged away the wooden cubicle, and the crude wooden seat.

"Bloody hell," he cursed, recoiling.

Why does shit have to smell so? he wondered. You would have thought that in the twenty first century they would have invented a pill to sweeten the smell. They put men on the bloody moon, created bombs of indescribable destruction, a pill for this and a pill for that, but no pill for shit smelling.

Eric smiled to himself.

Pity I can't share my thoughts with someone, he thought. Maybe one day I will tell the truth to Amy.

He filled in the hole with lime; straight away the smell lessened. Now all there was left was to dig a fresh hole.

"I have warm water waiting for you Eric in that pitcher," Amy called. "Please wash outside, and then splash some of my perfumed lavender water on you."

Bloody henpecked already, he thought, as he washed in the warm water. But I do like being pampered.

He bridled Beth, lifted Noah on her back, instructed him to grab her mane and then walked him round the paddock that was at the rear of the cottage. It was difficult to talk to Noah about battles that were fought, knights and weaponry. He was at that inquisitive age; he listened to other children and sees them wielding a wooden sword in mock battles. He always wanted Eric to tell him stories. He never knew what to say, only replying with, 'I'll tell you another time'.

He expected this would happen as the lad got older, and someday he knew he would have to discretely get as much information from the prior and his friends in the village as to the crusades, and local skirmishes, so that Noah wouldn't think him a right nerd when he asked. Amy, on the other hand, was very good at telling him bedside stories. On the odd occasion, Eric would tell him about Jack and the beanstalk and make it last for weeks on end.

That couldn't change history, a little story, could it? Eric had thought, as he still told the story.

Eric had to be up and Beth saddled early, as it was market day. The prior wanted Eric to take the market stall fees as they arrived from Derby. Thomas would direct stallholders onto the field, where they would erect tents or shelters of canvas. Two stable boys from the monastery would direct the traders horses' and carts in the adjacent field. The churchyard was to be used for the many stalls. The prior hoped that it was big enough to accommodate them all.

Amy and Noah were to follow on the traders' carts from the village, along with their precious vegetables. There was a sprinkle of summer rain as Eric positioned himself on the approach road to the church, not enough to dampen the day he hoped; at least it would keep the dust down. It's just as well he had looked up the coinage in use in this century before he had left. The local traders mainly used pennies or swapped items of equal value, however, larger denomination coins were in usage. The Royal Noble was worth one hundred and twenty pence, or ten shillings. The Noble was worth eighty pence, or six shillings and eight pence. Then there were the leopard coin and the helm, but it seemed these coins were mainly used by high status persons. Eric hadn't seen any of them in the thirteenth century.

Today he would mostly be dealing with would be half groats (worth tuppence) pennies. Eric had change never the less, in his pouch, given him by the prior. He could hear the rattle of carts behind him that told him the village traders were entering the designated areas. The carts started to arrive from Derby en masse; he stood in the centre of the road, accepted the penny given and explained as to where they should go. Not before stating that there were no weapons allowed beyond this point, of course. Travellers hitching a ride on the carts, walking, or arriving by horse, were welcome free of charge.

By midday, Eric was relieved by a monk from the monastery and handed over the money pouch to him. The sun was drying out the ground after the rain, which had stopped a few hours earlier. It was getting dusty again as Eric sauntered back down the road. When Eric was unoccupied as he was now, hands in pockets, placing one foot in front of the other, he always began to think of the things he missed. Simple things, like a mug of his mam's tea; coffee; a decent beer; his mates; bacon and eggs; and, of course, his parents. The endless trudge to the dole office every fortnight.

He hadn't made much of his life back home, if truth be known. There had been no job, no steady girlfriend – only his hobby and look where that'd got him. A century that stinks of shit all the time, hard work and very little to show for it; the clothes he wore were laughable.

But, Eric my lad, that's life, his inner conscious was telling him. You don't have another, so make the best of what you've got. I do love Amy and Noah and I'm sure I can better myself, but I do so much want to tell someone the truth about me. Maybe I will start by telling Amy, first.

After searching the numerous stalls, he finally found Amy. She had displayed the vegetables on a wide plank of wood, supported by two empty barrels. Noah was happily sucking on a sugar stick Amy had bought him.

"Well," Eric said, taking in the wares on her plank, "sold much?"

"As a matter of fact I have," replied Amy. "Look." She showed him the pennies in her hand. "And I have been complimented on the way I have displayed them, all washed and clean of dirt, and top and tailed just as you said I should."

"Would you mind, sweetheart, if I took a look around the stalls?" Eric asked. I will be back in no-time. Then you can go and spend as much time as you like."

"Alright," she said.

Eric knew exactly what he was looking for and hoped he had enough coins in his pouch to purchase them. He found the local blacksmith's stall.

"Afternoon Mathew" Eric said. "How's trade?

Eric thought Mathew was one of the kindest, gentle giants in the village.

"Hello Eric, how's that Amy – and young Noah?"

"Both fine, Mathew, thanks."

"Now what is it your're after, Eric?" Mathew asked. "Trade's a bit slow as you asked, but it's only the first day."

"Do you have by chance a griddle iron and stand?"

"As a matter of fact, I does. Ideal for fish, Eric."

"Thanks Mathew, I have other ideas for it," he grinned. "And a pan , not too big."

Eric paid, and bid him good day.

Next on his agenda was to buy some meat, beef steaks if he could get some. They were a rare commodity in this part of the country, due to cost to rear beef cattle, however, the monastery had dairy cows for the making of cheese and salted butter. He found a butcher's stall. The portly man in charge, arms covered in blood from hands to elbow, told him there was no beef so he settled for lamb; he received a queer look from the man, as Eric explained just how the steaks should be, and bought a few bacon strips. He then bought mushrooms, and finally some mixed spices and a jar of preserved plums, from the monastery's variety of fruit trees.

Whilst he was at the stall, he asked the young novice monk for a sweet bottle of mead, thinking it more palatable than beer. The stall was crammed with a vast variety of produce home grown from the monastery, from different kinds of beer, buttermilk, butter, cheeses, wines. From the bulge in the lad's money pouch he seemed to be doing well, but he did have competition from the Derby tradesmen, who were selling imported products. Eric wanted to know more about mead, he had never heard of it until he had some at his wedding.

"Well," the novice explained, "it's made from honey and water, and a little hops. Various spices are thrown in and left to ferment. It can be dry-sweet, or as strong as beer. The bottle you have has raisins in the top – when they were put in, they would sink to the bottom, and when they popped to the top we knew it was ready for drinking."

I learn something new every day in this period in time, Eric thought.

He thanked the novice and made his way back to Amy.

"What is that under your arm?" Amy asked, puzzled.

"Something for the evening meal, my dearest."

"And that bottle, and those packages?" Amy quizzed him.

"Look, get yourself and Noah away now," he said. "We will be leaving for home soon, and I have to go and see the monk on the Derby road before the market closes for the night."

Left alone by his stall, Eric began to dream again.

As markets go, this is basically no difference to ours back home, he decided.

"Are you going to sell me these goods or not?"

"I am so sorry," Eric said. "I was day dreaming."

He looked at a very old woman, bent forward with a back problem.

"What would you like, dear?" Eric asked, sounding as if he had been selling all his life.

"One onion, one turnip and one carrot, that's all as I want. How much?"

Eric hadn't got a clue, Amy hadn't told him the prices and he hadn't thought to ask.

"Tell you what, have the meal on me."

"I have to cook it first – and it would be a waste of good food if I have to pour it over your head," she said with a toothless grin.

Eric had no paper, or bag to put them in; the old woman stood looking at him.

"Here," she said, and lifted up her apron, which already had items in. Eric placed the vegetables alongside.

"How much?" she said again.

"Nothing, mother, you can have them for free."

"Ta very much," she said, and ambled away.

Of course they wouldn't understand the phrase, 'have it on me,' you stupid bugger, Eric thought to himself.

Slipping back into the dreaming mode again, he realized what was needed in this market.

A few of the people had baskets, but no, Bags. Shopping bags. I would make a killing, he thought. I could put a gold letter M for Middleton on the front. No, come to think of it, it would look a bit like 'Morrison's'. I suppose it would change history. Imagine having a Morrison's supermarket plastic bag in this century, now that would need a lot of explaining! He had to laugh at that.

The market was packing up for the day, the traders who needed to go back to restock were given a token, so they could return without payment. Amy returned to the stall with a grumpy Noah in tow.

"What's wrong with him?" Eric asked.

"Nothing really," explained Amy. "He was happy playing Knights, wielding his wooden sword with the other children, until I dragged him away."

"Would you like to ride back home with me, on Beth?" he asked Noah. "If that's alright with your mother."

"That's fine by me," she said. "As long as you two help me take the stall back to the village cart."

Seeing Amy safely on the cart, Eric gave her a kiss on the lips, which caused the other occupants on the cart to cheer.

"Won't be long," he said. "Remember to put the meat, buttermilk, and butter on the cold slab," he added, as an afterthought.

With Noah perched on his shoulder, Eric made for the top road.

"I have given all the tradesmen a token that have left the market, so as they can return free on the morrow," the monk explained to Eric as he approached. "The prior will be pleased with the takings today," he said, patting the money pouch.

"You might as well call it a day," said Eric. "Did you come by horse?"

"Yes," the monk answered, pointing to the meadow.

"Be sure to hand over the takings to brother Esop," Eric shouted over his shoulder, as he made his way over to Beth.

Eric had saddled up the horse in no time, swung Noah up, and mounted himself. Beth didn't need persuading as to which way to go.

Knowing she would be fed at her final destination she walked on that little bit faster. This gave Eric time to ponder whether to except prior Gilbert's offer of being a priest. He was suddenly brought out of his thoughts by Noah wielding his wooden sword in a high swishing movement, forcing Eric to dodge each swing.

On arrival at the cottage, Amy came out to greet them.

"What took you so long?" she said, grinning.

"You will have to take that up with old Beth," Eric chided.

"Can I go and see my friends?" Noah pleaded.

"It's dusk now," Eric intervened. "Dinner will soon be on the table."

"*Please* Dad!" Noah pleaded, Noah was advanced for his age, and Eric had no worries regarding Noah playing outside.

Once inside, Eric began to prepare their meal. First, he got the fire hot and placed the griddle over the embers, then he made the sauce using the salted butter, chopped mushrooms, a little flour, a chopped onion, and finally the herbs. With the sauce made, he emptied the plums into three wooden bowls, topping each with a dollop of buttermilk.

"I'm not late, am I Dad?"

"No son, you're right on time."

When he had them sitting at the table, he grilled the lamb steaks; job done, he covered each pewter plate with the sauce, cut the bread and they began to eat.

"Wine, I forgot the wine!" Eric exclaimed and opened the bottle, pouring a little amount for Noah, and larger measures for himself and Amy.

After dinner and with plates empty, Amy declared that it was the best meal she had ever tasted; little Noah agreed.

"How about you doing all the meals, Amy asked".

"That was a one off, besides, it was to show my appreciation to you both, and how much I love you."

With Noah in bed, Eric thought this was the right time to explain his past to Amy.

How do I begin? he thought.

CHAPTER SEVEN

"Amy my love, I have something very important to tell you," Eric hesitated, not quite sure how to put it.

"You are beginning to scare me now, Eric, please come out with it, whatever it is you have to say," said Amy, worried. "Is it about Noah, or prior Gilbert ?"

"No it's not about them," he told her. "It's about me and my past. You know I would never, ever lie to you my love. You will find what I have to say very disturbing and somewhat farfetched, but I swear by the holy script and the love of you and Noah, that what I am about to tell you is the truth."

He took a deep breath.

"I am from the future, Amy," he began. "I lived in Derbyshire, not too far from where we live today. The year was 2020. The year today is 1222 in the reign of the boy king, Henry III, but my sovereign was Queen Elizabeth II, some seven hundred and ninety eight years in the future. I was seventeen and my life was going nowhere. I had no employment, no girlfriend – I lived with my parents, but I had a pass-time Amy. A 'hobby' we called it, looking for buried artefacts in the ground, lost by people in centuries past.

"By some freak of nature, I found I was able to travel to a century belonging to a particular artefact that I had dug up from the ground," he said. "Living a short period of time in that century, then returning to my present time. In just a matter of months, I travelled backwards and forwards, not ageing, being able to speak the local dialect, and dressed in the local dress. But I had to lie, Amy, each time, like I did on coming amongst you and the villagers. If I hadn't I would be classed as someone dangerous or insane, and most probably killed if I hadn't."

Amy had that look of sheer bewilderment on her face, mouth open, eyes staring.

"Are you so shocked, my dearest Amy?" he asked her. "It's all true, and I know it is hard for you to take in, but I am glad that I have told you the truth. There will be no more lies, but we have to keep this between ourselves. You do understand that, don't you, Amy?"

She just stared at him, eyes as big as saucers, but she was not as ashen faced as she had been a few moments earlier.

"Say something, Amy," Eric begged, holding her hands in encouragement.

"Why don't you go back to your birth place?" she finally croaked the words.

"Because, Amy, stupid, stupid men damaged the Earth as we know it," he explained. "It's nothing but rubble and dust. I saw it for myself, when I last went back. But we are safe here, Amy. Also," he added, going a little pink. "I fell in love."

"This is not as a safe a place as you think, Eric," she said, after a moment. "It's uncertain and very dangerous – the throne keeps changing, bringing with it God knows what. One minute we're safe, the next we are taking up arms."

"I know that, but I am certain that I want to spend the rest of my life with you and Noah," he told her. "I will learn your ways of life, but I cannot change any part of it, except maybe help it along a little for the better."

"I have always felt a difference in you," said Amy. "The moment I first heard you speak, you were nothing like the village men. I loved you for it, as I love you now Eric, no matter where you came from."

"When I came through the church from my last journey, I witnessed a strange feeling coming over me, maybe it was because I dipped the coin in the font, and prayed at the altar," he said. "I was so desperate to find you, Amy. I swear it was the church that helped me find you, and because of that I have been considering taking the prior's offer of becoming a priest."

During the night they were wakened by thunder, followed by heavy rain and lightning. The rain sounded heavy enough to penetrate the thatch roof.

"We could have leaks by morning," Amy murmured, snuggling even closer to him.

"I hope Beth is dry," Eric said, sleepily.

It was still raining as dawn appeared; Amy placed a pail under one leak, in the centre of the room. Noah sat at the table, eyes still closed. Eric re-kindled the fire and put bacon in a pan over the embers, then whisked eggs and curd together with his knife.

"Oh to have a fork," he said to himself.

Bacon ready, he used the same pan for the eggs while Amy sliced the bread. Soon, they were ready to eat his scrambled eggs and bacon, washed down with sweet mead. Both Amy and Eric preferred mead to beer; Noah had milk, if it was not curdled, but drank mead at the evening meal.

Eric opened the door, the rain still coming down quite hard; he closed the door behind him, then dashed round to the stable. He was pleased to see that Beth was dry, and was happily munching on fresh hay that Arnold had given her.

"Morning, Arnold," Eric said, as Arnold was getting out the nights droppings.

"Morning, sir," he replied, looking like a drowned rat.

"When you have finished, pop indoors and Amy will give you some warm ale."

"That's very kind of you, sir," he answered. "Do you want me to saddle Beth up?"

"Not today thanks," Eric replied. "It's the least we can do – you look soaked to the skin."

He dashed back indoors, where Amy was clearing away the dishes and asked if she would heat some ale up for Arnold.

"Come on Noah, I will take you to school then go and see prior Gilbert," said Eric. "The children even at an early age were schooled by the monks".

Both huddled under a piece of canvas he got from the stables, he and Noah said their goodbyes to Amy.

The rain by now was malevolent and within seconds, they were both soaked down the front. Their clothes clung to the skin; very little shelter was given by the skimpy piece of canvas. The road, if you could call it that while it was actually more like a river, was awash with debris, horse shit, dog shit, and they also had to be aware of floating human turds. They reached the sanctuary of the monastery through the guarded gates, and dashed across the quadrangle to the shelter of the cloisters.

"Goodness me, you are wet, aren't you?" a passing monk remarked. "You will catch your death young boy."

"He's right, Noah," Eric said. "We need to change out of these sodden clothes and into something dryer, lead on to you classroom."

On reaching the room, Noah's teacher approached them, carrying bundles of wet clothes.

"Not another one," the elderly monk exclaimed. "We shall be running out of spare robes soon!"

He handed a robe to Noah.

"Go into the room boy, and slip those wet clothes off," he nodded at Eric. "I hope I can get them all dry by the end of the day."

Eric pondered with the idea of going home and seeing the prior another day, seeing as how drenched he was, but the job might be taken up if he dallied. Making up his mind to see him straight away, he sauntered off towards the prior's house. Since the door was not covered he was quickly drenched a second time. He knocked heavily on the oak door; a moment later it was opened by the same jumped up slimy git, keeping well inside the door, as not to get wet.

"What do you want?" He demanded "I would like to see the prior, please, if he is in residence," Eric said with gritted teeth.

"I wouldn't think the prior would see a dishevelled person, looking like you do," he said, acidly.

Eric leaned forward and grabbed a handful of the novice's grey habit. He pulled him outside into the rain.

"Listen to me, you slimy piece of pig shit, I have tried to be civil to you, but in return you have not," he snarled. "If I ever become a person of note I will have you shovel shit from the gutters for a week. Now go and get the bloody prior, who asked me to have a word next time I was here!"

He flung the wet canvas at him. Finally Eric was shown the door to prior Gilbert's study.

"Welcome Eric, come in," said prior Gilbert. "Is it raining that badly? Go and fetch a clean, dry towel from the linen cupboard," he gestured to the novice. "Then you can go about your duties. Please discard your shirt and top garments Eric. Come, sit by the fire."

273

Eric dried himself as best he could with the towel he was given and sat opposite the prior in front of the fire, where his hose began steaming.

"Well, Eric, what can I do for you?" he chuckled. "It's not often I entertain guests in my study, half naked."

"It's about the vacancy for the position of a priest in the parish," Eric stammered, from cold and nerves.

"Are you applying then?"

"Well, yes I am – if it's not already taken."

"No it is available, and I am so glad it is you applying, Eric," said the prior. "I will submit your acceptance to the Bishop today. Even if the weather is bad, I will send one of my envoys without delay, and he will wait for the Bishops approval. In the meantime, I would like to explain the fundamentals of the post. Not today, Eric – let's say on the morrow, around ten of the clock."

The prior summoned his novice.

"Would you please get the new priest his garments, and see him out?"

Eric bade his friend farewell and, as he sidled past the novice, he winked and put a finger to his temple.

"See, God moves in mysterious ways," he said to a dumbfounded novice.

The rain petered out to a fine drizzle as he neared the cottage, but he still had to dodge the filth on the road.

Wellington boots would be the order of the day, he thought as he pushed open the door.

Dressed in a change of clothes, Eric began scribbling down a list of questions he wanted to put to the prior, using charcoal on a piece of parchment.

"Will you carry out your threat to the novice?" Amy asked.

"I doubt there is need now," Eric replied. "Although it would be nice to wipe that surly, smug look off his face."

With breakfast over, Noah left to walk to school with friends. The weather was fine, a big difference to yesterday. Eric decided he would take Beth out; it would be a little exercise for her. He rode slowly, but he was still early.

"Am I doing the right thing?" he asked himself. "What else can I do? We need the money, and with training I might be good at it."

He went through the gates.

One guard said, "Morning preacher," and the other just grinned.

"I haven't got the job yet," he said to them, but they clearly thought it was in the bag. He noticed a large war horse tethered outside the prior's house; Eric dismounted, and tethered Beth alongside it.

Nobility? Eric pondered. The horse was draped in fine livery colours. He hesitated before knocking. This is it, he thought. The job centre couldn't find me a job, yet here I am applying for a job as a priest in the twelfth century.

The novice bade him in with a slight bow of the head.

Makes a bloody change, Eric thought, as he followed him. *I must stop swearing,* Eric chided himself, and smiled.

"Come in Eric," the prior greeted him with a handshake. "Of course you have met Lord Wilfred, have you not?"

Eric shook hands with him and they all sat.

"My envoy came back with a message for me
Eric, and he, the Bishop, says," he began to read
from the parchment on his desk, "'If you
recommend this man for being the priest of
Moorcroft, then I will, at this point, agree with
your judgement. However, you are aware that
the Lord of the manor also has to agree with
your choice. If he is in agreement, then I will be
only too pleased to train the man. Please give
me the impending dates of his arrival'. So, there
you have it gentlemen," the prior concluded.
"All that is left is for your Lordship to interview
Eric in my presence, and to decide upon the
appointment."

Lord Wilfred cleared his throat with a cough.

"I attended your wedding Eric, along with my
sons, but we didn't have time to talk at length.
However, you did well at the theft of the stone.
You used your initiative, and I am led to believe
you keep a good set of books. I have to pose
this next question to you Eric," he continued.
"With the rebels close to knocking on our door
in outrage to the land taxes, would you Eric,
take up arms."

"To defend the village and parish in a just cause, then yes," Eric gave his answer.

"That is a good enough answer for me, prior, I agree to his application," said Lord Wilfred, satisfied. "Now, if you will excuse me gentlemen, I have work to do in Derby. Congratulations, Eric," his Lordship said, as he left the room.

"That went well, don't you think?" a jubilant prior exclaimed. "We have a priest at last, 'but I do have to explain the fundamentals of the post to you Eric, even though I explained the role of being a priest some months ago'. Your salary comes from the church and not me, or should I say the monastery, it is from the parish lands, i.e. services carried out by you for a fee on, weddings, funerals, baptisms, and of course the Tithe money, $1/10^{th}$ of a person's earnings to support the church, divided between yourself, the church main'tenance, funds for the poor, and not forgetting the Bishop, he and I will discuss your salary Eric. The moneys by the people will be collected in the nave of the church, and courts headed by his Lordship, will also be held in the nave, whether civil or criminal.'That Eric, sums it up briefly, 'now' is there some questions you wish to put to me'."

 "Yes" Eric began, "do you honestly believe I will make a good priest, because I haven't been a good church goer in my life, and there is an awful lot to take in."

"I can judge a good man in battle, or otherwise. I came up through the ranks, so to speak, and yes, Eric, I do think you will make a good priest."

"Right," said Eric, accepting this. "What's next? I know I have to go for training, but what do I wear. Before I venture further Eric, there is something I must tell you. The church is moving towards a celibate priesthood without family. But, until that arises, we will carry on. 'The prior so wanting a priest soonest'.

"You will wear the monastic dress Eric, a simple habit and a simple belt," the prior explained. "Under canon law, you are required to wear plain, sober clothes in your daily life. However, in service it will be a long sleeved tunic, called a Dalmatic – as long as it reaches the feet. It is in contrast to the hose and bare legs of laymen."

"Thank you, sir, just one final question," said Eric. "Can I have an input on the construction of the parsonage?"

"Of course you can, my dear Eric, but the siting must be as close to the church as is possible, and the cost of the build is from the diocese. It will begin as soon as you leave for Derby."

Eric's head was bursting from all the information that had been fed to him.

Can I do it? he kept repeating to himself, as he headed home. Why not? I'm alive, after all, which is more than can be said of the poor buggers I left behind.

"Well?" Amy said as he entered the kitchen.

"Just give me a minute, Amy. I need to get my head clear, and then I will tell you all."

"When do you go to Derby, then?" Amy asked.

"I'm not sure, the prior said he will let me know soon," he said. "What I need to do is sketch a drawing of the house for Thomas and the men who are going to build it. I want a slate roof, not thatch, and stone floors; glass windows, plenty of rooms, and –"

"Slow down, Eric my love," Amy laughed. "I understand you are excited, but eat first. I have cheese and bread on the table, and I will get you parchment and charcoal."

When Noah came in from school, Eric began to explain the job to the lad, but above all why he had to go away.

"Will they teach you how to fight, as well? Noah asked.

"No, not really, but I guess they would if I asked," replied Eric, swinging Noah by his arms, and kissing him at the same time.

It was that evening, snuggling up under the covers in bed, that Amy dropped a bombshell of a request on Eric, that could have devastating results if carried out.

"I want to go and see where you were born," she said. "I have tried and tried to believe you, my dearest, and I know you wouldn't lie to me, but my heart is not whole, and I want us to be one with each other."

"I know it must be hard for you Amy to fully understand, but I came through with the silver sixpence as I have explained to you, I am not

281

sure if it will work with two people, and we may never get back again, if it works at all."

"Have faith, Eric," she told him. "As you said, it was the church that brought you back to me and Noah."

"Let me think about it, Amy," he said. "I will make a decision in the morning."

How could he sleep now, with all those thoughts racing around in his head? Amy was so determined, and yet the possibility of failure was so likely – could he put her through it? And then there was Noah to consider. Eric tried to imagine the possibilities.

The radioactive fallout dust on the surface could, by now, be weather diluted, given the years I have been away, he thought. Would the coin work with two? Would Noah end up an orphan?

Breakfast was quiet between Eric and Amy; Noah chattered on, as he normally did, but he sensed the tension in the room.

"Are you going to Derby today, Dad?" Noah's question broke the silence.

"Not today, son, maybe in a few days' time," Eric answered the lad.

"Well?" Amy asked Eric, after Noah left for school. "Have you made a decision?"

"Yes and no," Eric said. "I wanted to put a few questions to you before I do. Would Eleanor and Seth look after Noah if – and I say if – we don't find our way back?"

"I'm sure they would," Amy confirmed, not liking the question at all.

"Alright, and secondly, would you explain to Noah why his father didn't come back, if it only works for me and not you?"

"Of course I would, I would explain that you went away for a while, and to the prior I would say you got cold feet, and needed to go away and think."

"Very well then, if you are still determined my love, we will try today," he told her. "But first, go and see your friend Eleanor and ask her if she would pick Noah up from school. I, in the meantime, will see if a cart is leaving for Derby from the village, to get a ride to the church. Tell your friend we are going shopping for items to put in the new house."

At 10 a.m. that morning, they were perched on a cart, bound for Derby. They jumped down as the driver slowed down for them at the church; they thanked him, and watched as he disappeared out of sight, before making their way to the cess pit in the corner of the field. The stink was not as rife as when the market had last been there, but Amy still pinched her nose together.

"Is this the place?" she asked.

"Yes," Eric said, making the ground comfortable for Amy.

For the first time in ages, Eric took notice of Amy's attire: her little white coif cap, the ties hanging down; her grey dress, white linen collar, and simple shoes; a canvas bag hung loosely by hemp across her shoulders and down to her hip. On impulse he drew her close in an embrace, and kissed her.

"I love you, milady," Eric said.

"It's not the best of romantic places, is it?" Amy said, putting a hand over her mouth again.

They lay down as close together as they could, the silver sixpence in Eric's hand.

"Hold a corner of the coin," he told Amy. "Rub it and close your eyes, and believe. Now."

It worked, Eric gasped as he took in the sensation of being in the drift mine. Amy was a little dazed, but otherwise in one piece, and – Eric noticed, in the same attire – yet he was back in his jeans and jacket. His holdall were he left it; just enough light was penetrating the entrance. Amy was speechless; she just looked at Eric in bewilderment, and gave a little giggle.

"You look so silly in those clothes and that," she pointed at his bag.

"I will tell you later," he said. "We must try and get out."

They were like two moles appearing from underground; Eric immediately took stock of the surroundings, the dust was caked hard, now. The sky was clear of the grey blanket that had seemed so dense before; a feeble sun tried to penetrate through a few dense clouds.

"So far, so good," he said to Amy, as she clung on his arm.

"Your speech is different Eric, you talk funny, but learned – has mine changed?"

"No," Eric replied. "Come, we must not linger. The less time we are here the better."

They walked by the church, past the disused farm, and onto the road. It was so quiet, Eric observed, ever looking around him. Eventually, after a good hour of walking, Amy insisted on resting. She didn't have the pace Eric had, due to her long skirt and thin shoes.

"We are nearly there now," he said and slowed the pace.

They passed a corner shop, the windows still intact, but empty. Then they arrived at his house. What roofs were left on the street were covered in a layer of grey silt; the garden gate was off its hinges. The trees were bare – there were no birds, the place was so desolate.

"Do you want to enter the building?" Amy asked.

"No," he said, after a moment. "I wouldn't like what I might see."

"Strange dwellings," Amy said. "What are those stones sticking up?"

"Those, my dearest, are chimneys to take away the smoke from the fires within."

He looked around, and for the first time Eric noticed a scattering of cars, all covered in the grey slime.

"We must make our way back, Amy. I will answer all your questions at a later time."

Eric was frightened of the eerie place, as if they were the only ones alive in it, and someone would jump out at them, all disfigured, like the living dead. On passing the shop, Eric went back to peer in at the window; he couldn't see beyond the grime so he pushed open the door – what was left of it – and stepped inside. Amy followed, clinging to him.

He had trouble identifying things that were not broken, but he did find a jar of coffee and a box of tea bags, and put them in Amy's bag. Outside Eric noticed blue smoke curling upwards, and guessed it to be about a mile away.

So we aren't the only ones here, he said to himself.

Amy was exhausted by the time they reached the church; Eric wanted to put a greater distance between them and the smoke. Going inside, Amy was beside herself.

"Eric look, it's just like Thomas's build!"

"It is Thomas's build," Eric said. "Apart from the altar and seating, it's the same. Come on," he said, and led Amy outside. "Look," he said, pointing to the initials 'EM'. "I did that when the church was finished, I borrowed Anthony's tools."

Eric knew he was on borrowed time, so he quickly marched Amy along the back of the church, to show her their grave. She started shaking, and wished to leave.

"Yes," Eric agreed, "but I need to dip the coin in what little water is left in the font."

Amy stayed outside while Eric nipped inside, put the coin through the dregs, and prayed.

Back in the mine, Eric showed her the money he had in his bag and the other relics he had found, along with his metal detector, and spade.

"I wonder," Eric said aloud, "if those items in your bag will be transported with us. My watch was."

"I don't understand, Eric."

"You will later," he said. "Now, stand close to me with your back against the wall, hold a corner of the coin, and close your eyes. Ready?" he asked. "Now."

"The sensation didn't seem quite so bad with two of us," he said, as he lay with Amy, not daring to open his eyes.

"Has it worked?" she said breathlessly.

"I don't know yet, I haven't opened my eyes, but I can smell the shit from the cess pool," he said, then apologised for swearing. "Sorry. One, two, three – open."

Eric stood, followed by Amy. He looked around. They were standing beside the cess pit, a little way from the church.

"I think we are back, Amy," he said, pleased. "Just to make sure, go and see if there are any graves back there."

Amy ran as fast as she could and was soon back.

"No graves," she said.

"Then we are definitely back, my love," he told her. "Look at me, my clothes are normal."

"And you speak like me, Eric."

"There is something I have to do, before we go home," he said. Eric took the silver sixpence and buried it as best he could, beside the cess pit.

"Maybe, just maybe," he said. "Someone in the near future just might dig this up."

They began the walk home.

"How do you feel, Amy?" Eric asked. "No dizziness, itching, feeling sickly?"

"No," she said, surprised. "Why the questions?"

"Travelling through the wall can make you feel funny," he said, but the real reason for the questions was the possibility of radiation sickness.

As they neared the village, the stench hit them.

"Strange there being no smells in your world, my love," remarked Amy.

"It's good to be back," laughed Eric.

After supper was finished and Noah was tucked up for the night, Eric remembered the coffee and tea in Amy's bag. Amy produced the items from her bag. Eric just sat and stared at them on the table for quite some time, before finally he jumped up and set a pan of water on the embers.

"What are those brown crystals and these little pouches?" Amy asked, taking a teabag from the box gingerly. "Why do they mean so much to you, Eric?"

"These, love, are what I have been dreaming of for centuries," he laughed. "This is called 'coffee'," he told her, pointing to the jar. "And these little gems are called 'tea'. They are beverages we drank in my time."

Pouring hot water over the tea bag in the tankard, adding a smidgeon of honey and a little milk, he inhaled the fumes, happily.

"That, my love, is pure nectar."

He let Amy sniff the brew; she screwed up her nose in dislike. Holding the pewter mug in his hands, Eric sipped his tea and exhaled content.

"Now, my love, I am ready to take on the world."

Author's Note

The village in Derbyshire is purely fictitious, however, if it seems correct, then it's simply a coincidence. The History facts were taken from Google.

ACKNOWLEDGEMENT

To my wife, Veronica, for her patience and input, but especially in her time of illness, when she was my ardent critic.

Also to my daughter, Theresa, and son, Clive, for their input in saying: "Haven't you finished it yet?"

To my Cousin Alan Collier for his work on the book cover.

16602030R00167

Printed in Poland
by Amazon Fulfillment
Poland Sp. z o.o., Wrocław